THE YEAR OF THE
BULL

OSCAR PARLAND

THE YEAR OF THE
BULL

TRANSLATED
FROM THE SWEDISH
BY JOAN TATE

PETER OWEN
LONDON & CHESTER SPRINGS PA

PETER OWEN PUBLISHERS
73 Kenway Road London SW5 0RE

Peter Owen books are distributed in the USA by
Dufour Editions Inc. Chester Springs PA 19425–0449

Translated from the Swedish *Tjurens år*
© Oscar Parland 1962, 1988
English translation © Joan Tate 1991
First published in Great Britain 1991

*The illustrations on p.199 and on the
endpapers are from wood engravings by
Thomas Bewick*

British Library Cataloguing in Publication Data
Parland, Oscar, 1912–
The year of the bull.
I. Title
839.7374

ISBN 0–7206–0807–4

Typeset in Melior by Selectmove London W3
Printed in Great Britain by Billings of Worcester

The world bathes in blood so that
God may live.

EDITH SÖDERGRAN

PREFACE

(From a lecture given by Oscar Parland at Helsinki University in 1968 on how his books came about.)

MY FATHER'S FAMILY COMES FROM ENGLAND. MY paternal great-great-grandfather moved to St Petersburg in the days of Katarina II. According to family tradition, he became language tutor to the future Tsar, Alexander, and his brother Konstantin. His heirs became resident in the Russian capital. My paternal grandfather was a stockbroker and became a Finnish subject, because he approved of Finland's liberal and Western laws, but he spent all his life in St Petersburg. Some members of the family had artistic inclinations, collected works of art, drew and painted as a hobby and often stayed in Italy. One of my great-uncles was Professor of Architecture and built the Church of Edification in St Petersburg in memory of the assassination of Alexander II. One of my father's brothers died at twenty-one in mysterious circumstances in a shooting accident and left behind him a fragment of a novel in Russian which was published in 1912, a tale of unhappy love and jealousy reminiscent of Lermontov's *A Hero of Our Time* and my brother's *Broken*.

My mother, née Sesemann, came from Viborg of a family of German merchants who settled there after the Thirty Years War. My maternal grandfather trained as a doctor in Helsinki but later went to live in St Petersburg as Chief Medical Officer of Finnish Railways. (St Petersburg was at the time the terminal station for Finnish trains running eastwards.) My mother was German-Baltic from Livland. Her father was a priest in St Petersburg. So both my parents grew up in what was at the time the capital of Russia and were at home in the cosmopolitan bourgeois milieu of Baltic-German-English-Finnish extraction, influenced by the Russian atmosphere. My father was a diplomat-engineer and served with the Russian State Railways. I myself was born in Kiev. The connection with Finland consisted mainly of relations with the Sesemann estate in Tikkala near Viborg, where my parents used to spend part of the summer with my maternal grandparents' large family. After my grandfather died, my grandmother and my mother and we children moved to Tikkala and lived there all the year round from 1914 to the end of 1919. My father stayed in St Petersburg and came to see us at weekends and during holidays. I have no memory of the first two years of my life. To me, my life started at Tikkala. I remember very well indeed the end of the world that came with the Russian Revolution. The protected and idyllic world of my childhood collapsed. We lost everything we possessed except the provisionally equipped house and our share of the modest little estate, which turned out to contain thirty-seven relations. The thirty-seven uncles and aunts invaded the estate as refugees from the Revolution, occupied the summer houses round about and made their demands known. Naturally it proved impossible for them to live and support themselves in this way. They lived in misery and quarrelled, most of them gradually moving away and selling their houses, others staying and a few becoming in time anachronistic Chekhovian eccentrics. For a while things were very difficult and we lived on allowances from foreign women friends of my grandmother's and the American aid organizations. At the outbreak of the Civil War, we were cut off from our father and had no help from him. Not until 1921 did he manage to get over the border. He eventually found employment with the Railway Board in Helsinki. But as his Finnish was deficient, he was never able to find employment corresponding to his qualifications.

In 1922 we moved via Kilo to Grankulla, but we still spent the summers in Karelia, in Kellomäki or

Tikkala. Although my father was a Finnish citizen, we were regarded as Russian emigrants. This was due to our wretched finances and also to my parents' deficiencies in both of the languages of the country. I remember the feeling of social degradation that characterized my relations with my school friends. Henry, who was almost four years older than I was, must have felt this much more strongly. At the time, everything Russian was extremely unpopular and the animosity towards our Russian origins could take on arrogant forms among our contemporaries. I think these experiences from childhood have had a lasting influence on my attitude to life. I deeply distrust all static constructions of ideas and axioms, however attractive they may be. Heraclitus' view that all things move and are transformed is fundamental to my attitude. I have tried to give this form in my books.

I must emphasize one circumstance that is important in my writing, my polyglotism. As long as I can remember, I have spoken Russian and German. Then Finnish was added, thanks to my contact with the workers' children at Tikkala and at primary school. Our spoken language at home was German, and German remained the language of conversation between us brothers right up to senior school, but we also spoke Russian – our father in particular when he was excited or upset. In the early days at Tikkala I heard the adults speaking Swedish, but I did not learn Swedish until I was ten, when I started at Grankulla School. Nowadays Swedish is the language I am most proficient in and Finnish has become my second language, while Russian and German have faded away. But I still cannot say which language I use when I am thinking – I really think simultaneously in all those languages. German was the natural medium for me when I was expressing myself in writing up until I was fifteen, and my first literary attempts were in German, though nowadays I find it quite difficult to write a letter in German. Unfortunately, I must say that Swedish still causes me some difficulties not only when it concerns grammatically correct sentence construction but in the use of actual words; most troublesome are the words that in my mind are often in Russian, German or Finnish. A lot of energy goes into translating a word or an expression into Swedish, and I often find that the expression generally speaking has no Swedish equivalent.

If I were to write down words just as they come into my mind, then the writing would always switch between four different languages. It would be a kind of code language in the style of Joyce's *Finnegans Wake*. So I have to stick to Swedish and console myself that there are other authors who have changed language. Perhaps a certain insecurity and lack of knowledge of the conventionally correct expressions and clichés have contributed to this many-faceted treatment of language.

THERE'S BEEN WAR AS LONG AS I CAN REMEMBER.
When we say our prayers at night with Grandmother,
we're never allowed to forget the War. That the War will
eventually come to an end is even more important than
that the Papuans are baptized or that every night God
takes all the uncles and aunts under his protection. I don't
really believe it can ever end, because it's always existed.
All the same, every night we have to remind God about the
War, so that he doesn't forget it – perhaps he'll find a way
to end it somehow. At least that's what Grandmother and
the other Grown-ups think.

The War can't be seen or heard. You can see it only
on pictures, but all the same it's always around us, so
the Grown-ups can't help talking and worrying about
it the whole time. You can see the War in books and
magazines: soldiers and knights, kings and marshals
on foot or on horseback, perched on elephants, on
chariots or the backs of trucks, with fluttering flags
and standards, with shining sabres and lances, with
rifles and cannons. They are all fighting each other,
so that it's one great throng and at first you can't
distinguish the screaming faces, the raised arms or
the kicking legs from each other or work out to whom
they belong. When you look down at the ground under
the horses' hoofs and the warriors' spurs, you find the
dead and the wounded being trampled to pieces by
the fighters. They're bleeding from horrible wounds
and being chopped to bits and maimed, holding up
their arms and crying for help. The grass round them

11

is blood-stained and the ground covered with glistening red pools.

'The world is being drowned in blood,' Grandmother says.

When I think about the War and close my eyes, I see rivulets trickling through the grass. They never stop, because as soon as the dying have been drained of all their blood and breathed their last, scores more rush forward and drop down dead beside the other dead. Blood gurgles out everywhere from bubbling springs. The ground can't absorb it, the streams run into creeks, the creeks into rivers, and the rivers grow – soon the battlefield is one great lake in which the living and the dead swirl round in the dark red waves. In the end, it must overflow and become like the Deluge. The wave of blood will wash over our windows, rise above the chimney- and tree-tops and finally cover the top of King's Mountain. How shall we be able to save ourselves then?

This War business must have already begun when people decided to defy God and tried to build a tower that would reach right up to the clouds in order to be able to look into Heaven. They nearly succeeded. The tower was already just touching the bottom of the clouds – a tiny bit more and the people would have climbed up the backs of the clouds and looked at the wonders of Heaven. Then the mist parted round the top of the tower and God and the angels appeared with glittering swords in their hands. People's tongues were immediately *confounded* so they couldn't make themselves understood. Instead of going on building the tower, they started quarrelling and fighting. They took each other's tools, threw each other off the scaffolding and marched away, some in one direction, others in another. The tower of Babel was never finished.

Confounded is a strange word. It tastes bitter like quinine and you're afraid of biting your tongue when you try to say it. It must be an enchanted word with which God bewitches your tongue, making you open your mouth so wide you can't say words as before. Grandmother says that ever since then people have spoken different languages and divided themselves up into different peoples. The people don't understand each other and are always quarrelling and going into battle against each other. At first it was the Amalekites and the Ammonites and the Trilobites and lots more the children of Israel always had to fight against. After them came the Greeks and the Romans and the Nibelungs and the Knights of the Round Table, the Tartars and the Russians, King Charles XII and Napoleon, the Sultan and Münchhausen, whatever they are all called, for they're so many you can't possibly remember them all. Sometimes one of them won, sometimes the other, and all the time everything simply got worse and people found it harder and harder to agree. But things have never been so bad as they are now, Grandmother says, for everyone and every country in the whole world are fighting each other and never before has so much blood flowed.

They're the English and the Russians and the French and the Germans, the Americans and the Montenegrins and lots more I can't even remember. Grandmother and Mamma are on the side of the Germans and say they will win, because the Germans fear God. One fine day the English and the French and the Russians will be horribly punished for what they're doing now. The English are liars and unbelievers and the Russians and the French are swine. That must mean that the English always tell lies and cheat and that the Russians and French speak 'indecently' and do things it's forbidden to talk about or even think about. But Pappa likes the English and says they must resemble angels and be very beautiful. Things mustn't go wrong for them. French bread is good. How can I think badly of the French and how shall we manage if things go wrong for them? And then they're friends of Uncle Frans, too, and he's almost as old as Grandmother and lives in the Big House with its sky-high staircase. He's like God and will never allow the French to lose.

But Uncle Georg is on the side of the Russians. When he talks about the War with Grandmother, he at once goes red in the face and the white whiskers under his nose stick out as on a walrus. He rumbles and shouts: 'Nikolaschka will manage it! You'll see, Muscha, you'll see.'

Nikolaschka is the Tsar of Russia. Uncle Georg likes Nikolaschka and wants him to win. But Grandmother isn't frightened when Uncle Georg tries to scare her and waves his knobbly hands in the air. She just purses her lips and then says: 'Well, Georg my dear, how is your Nikolaschka going to get himself out of this mess?'

'Calm down, Muscha dear,' says Uncle Georg, digging into his trouser pocket and taking out his big check handkerchief. He wipes his bald head and goes on: 'We mustn't get too excited. Remember your heart.'

'But I'm perfectly calm,' says Grandmother.

'Wilhelm's a fool!' explodes Uncle Georg again. 'That's what I say – a dreamer, an ass, a prize idiot!' He turns on his heel and the door slams with a terrible bang, as if he had thought of hitting Wilhelm on the head with it.

Grandmother smiles with her mouth pursed and patters off to her room without saying anything. I'm afraid on Uncle Georg's behalf, because Grandmother likes this Wilhelm who is the Kaiser. She says 'Kaiser Wilhelm' and won't have anything said against him. It could be that not only the Tsar but also Uncle Georg will find himself in trouble if he goes on annoying Grandmother.

Before, the War was so far away you just didn't think about it. Sometimes when Pappa was at home, some tall uncle would appear in uniform with flashing buttons and epaulettes and gold tassels on the hilt of his sword. They came from St Petersburg and spoke Russian, kissed you on the cheek, laughed and lifted you up high above their heads. They were just as magnificent and unusual as the Two-tailed Pasha and some of the other wonderfully coloured creatures which on rare occasions appear in our garden. I was afraid to touch them in the way you're

afraid to touch anything beautiful and brand new, and I
went stiff all over when they held me. They walked round
our home in their brilliantly polished boots, their spurs
jangling, then suddenly disappeared, never to return.

The lovely happy aunts who speak Russian also
come more and more infrequently from Petersburg.
Recently they haven't put in an appearance at all.
They smelt so good and always brought presents for
us, camels and tigers, picture-books and boxes of sweets
tied round with blue or pink silk ribbon. When they
came to visit us, everything here at home was different.
They were so happy and talked and laughed so much,
you yourself were happy and started laughing without
knowing why. Sometimes they took you with them for
a walk and then they picked flowers and showed you
funny animals, beetles, butterflies and grasshoppers, and
told you their names.

Once two young aunts took me to the swing in the Big
House park. One of them took me in her arms and so all
three of us swung. We flew high up over the branches of
the trees, the grass below becoming streaky like rushing
water and the whole world seesawing and swinging
up and down. Sometimes the forests and mountains
disappeared below us, sometimes everything stood on
edge and almost tipped over on to us. The aunts'
pink and blue dresses were blown up like balloons,
sometimes against my face so that I could see nothing,
sometimes flapping aside so that I caught a glimpse of
their lovely shapely legs, their dark glistening stockings,
their suspenders and a piece of the white skin of their
thighs. And all the time they laughed and tried to swing
even higher and more wildly. I laughed too, for their hair
tickled my face and I had a funny feeling in my mouth
and stomach.

Afterwards we all three sat on a bench and one of
the aunts held me in her arms and the other tickled my
face with a long piece of grass and asked me whether
I wouldn't rather sit on her lap. I liked both of them

wanting me and squabbling over me. It was nice when the pink aunt held me tight and wouldn't let me go, but I also liked it when the blue one leant over and asked me if I would like to have a kiss – it was pale blue, she said, and the most beautiful in the whole world. So she gave me a pale blue kiss on the mouth. But then the other one gave me a pink kiss and asked me whether the pink one wasn't even more beautiful than the blue one. In my turn, I returned the kisses, a pale blue one to the one in blue and a pink one to the one in pink, and then we all gave each other different coloured kisses, yellow and green and purple and rainbow-coloured, and it was more and more fun. But then suddenly Uncle Bobbi came walking down the garden path and then the two aunts jumped up and rushed after him. I stayed behind on my own with all those green, yellow and red kisses dancing round me like dazzling spots of sunlight.

I miss all those aunts and uncles from Petersburg, not just because they were so lovely and happy, but also because everything was so different when they were here. They belonged with Pappa in some way, and when they were here, everything was exciting and fun, like at a party. Grandmother and Mamma and Aunt seemed to kind of fade into the background, weren't so noticeable – almost as if they weren't really real and Pappa became more and more tangible and larger, bewitching the whole household. The table was laden with delicious things; bowls of grapes and peaches, boxes of glittering green and red slices of limes and oranges went round, and Aunt came in with a huge water-melon or a mountain of melons on a dish. Pappa got up from his place to cut the juicy dripping fruit with a knife. Huge leopard-spotted fish appeared at the dinner-table embedded in vegetables and filled with rice and plums. Then came the dessert you'd been waiting for with such excitement: a trembling pale yellow jelly, a vanilla-flavoured blancmange, sago pudding, apple pie and on rare occasions a mountain of ice-cream, garnished with strawberries or grapes. You could feel yourself melting inside as the dish went round. Then Aunt gave you a helping. You tasted a little, taking only a tiny bit on the spoon so that the treasure wouldn't come to an end all too soon. The contents of the spoon had to melt slowly in your mouth before you swallowed.

In the evenings, the table glittered with wineglasses so that it looked like a flower-bed full of glass lilies. When Pappa uncorked the tall narrow bottle, the glasses tinkled faintly like bells chiming. Then the aunts and uncles danced with each other and Mamma or Pappa sat at the piano and played. Even when I was lying in bed, I could hear the aunts' ringing laughter, the strumming of the piano, feet scraping along the floor, and I could feel the whole house trembling below me.

Pappa seldom comes now. He has more and more lost the ability to bewitch our lives. Everything stays almost the same whenever he appears and he's become more and more distant and unreal. The delicious foods stay away just as obstinately as the happy Russian uncles and aunts with their presents. Sometimes you forget about it, but then you notice you're really thinking about good food all the time. You're always a little miserable, because you're never given anything that tastes really good; the happy excitement that seized you when you were at table is now gone, for you know you're going to be disappointed. It's as if I'd never tasted those wonderful dishes, as if it had all been a dream. I don't remember what they tasted like any longer, and can only just remember what they looked like.

It's quite different in my dreams. Then I walk around between dishes laden with grapes, oranges, peaches, cream cakes, whipped cream and ice-cream. Once I even dreamt about a great dish of mashed potatoes and smoked knackwurst sausages carried in for dinner one Sunday when Pappa was at home. The sad thing is I never get as far as tasting those lovely things in the dreams. At the last moment something unexpected happens, someone comes and takes the food away, the fruit and sweets, without my stopping them and I wake up. When I realize it's all been a dream, I'm so miserable my eyes smart and I get a lump in my throat. It doesn't help to press my face into my pillow and try to go back to sleep. Either I don't sleep at all or else I dream about something quite different.

When I once asked Grandmother why we never had anything good to eat, she said it was because of the War. All the grapes, the marzipan sweets and jars of honey have vanished because of the War. It's also the War's fault that the happy aunts from St Petersburg don't come to see us any longer and that we see Pappa so rarely. Everything that's miserable is because of the War. The Russian soldiers cutting down the forest and digging trenches over by the Viborg road and who stole the jars of preserves and butter from our cellar are also there because of the War.

'Why doesn't God put an end to the War?' I ask. 'We pray for it every night.'

'Because people are so wicked,' says Grandmother. 'God is punishing the people for forgetting him and living in sin and shame.'

'But doesn't he feel sorry for people?'

'No, Riki,' says Grandmother. 'They haven't been punished enough yet. God won't put an end to the War until people change their minds and start believing in him again.'

'But when will people change their minds so that the War ends?'

'I don't know. They haven't learnt anything yet. Day by day their wickedness grows and their misdeeds cry to the skies. It's getting worse than in Sodom and Gomorrah.'

'Then it'll always just get worse and worse?'

'Yes,' says Grandmother, nodding. 'It's getting worse and worse all the time.'

'But why do we have to pray to God to put an end to the War, if everything has to end badly anyhow?'

'Perhaps the last days aren't yet here,' says Grandmother, clasping her hands. 'Perhaps he will still take pity on people and allow them to live in another happier era. We must keep vigil and implore him for mercy so that the world is saved.'

On Sunday mornings, Grandmother reads about the Day of Wrath:

'And I saw when the Lamb opened one of the seals, and I heard, as it were the noise of thunder, one of the four beasts saying, Come and see.

'And I saw, and behold a white horse: and he that sat on him had a bow; and a crown was given unto him: and he went forth conquering, and to conquer.

'And when he had opened the second seal, I heard the second beast say, Come and see.

'And there went out another horse that was red: and power was given to him that sat thereon to take peace from the earth, and that they should kill one another: and there was given unto him a great sword.

'And when he had opened the third seal, I heard the third beast say, Come and see. And I beheld, and lo a black horse; and he that sat on him had a pair of balances in his hand.

'And I heard a voice in the midst of the four beasts say, A measure of wheat for a penny, and three measures of barley for a penny; and see thou hurt not the oil and the wine.

'And when he had opened the fourth seal, I heard the voice of the fourth beast say, Come and see.

'And I looked, and behold a pale horse: and his name that sat on him was Death, and Hell followed with him. And power was given unto them over the fourth part of the earth, to kill with sword, and with hunger, and with death, and with the beasts of the earth. . . .'

IN THE DRAWER OF GRANDMOTHER'S DESK THERE'S a coloured picture of an angel. He's lying on his back with his arm behind his head, obscured by a shower of broken peacock feathers. It's a postcard that has come from somewhere far away at the end of the world, because it's got a red stamp and is franked on the back. Aunt Luscha had it in her bag when she came to see Grandmother to talk about holy things. Grandmother and Aunt Luscha soon locked themselves inside Grandmother's room and not even Mamma was allowed in to disturb them. Afterwards, Grandmother and Mamma talked for ages about that postcard. Grandmother polished her glasses, put them on her nose and looked at the picture again. Then she sighed, shook her head and put it aside on her desk. They were speaking French all the time so that we wouldn't understand what they were saying.

The picture of the angel is both lovely and horrible at the same time. He's lying there tensing his naked body under the feather covering as if everything hurt very badly. His face is beautiful but nasty, stony with hatred, as if just about to bite. It scares you just to look at it.

When I asked Grandmother what the angel's name was and why he looked so nasty, she wouldn't tell me. But I gradually wheedled it out of her that his name was Lucifer.

At that time, God hadn't created the world or planted the Garden of Eden. There were no plants, no animals, no people – only silvery white clouds hovering above bottomless depths. God and the angels lived up there in an eternally radiant light. As far as anyone could see, the clouds piled up behind each other like a landscape of snow-covered mountains, and on top of them angels in full-length gowns knelt with harps and zithers in their hands. They flapped their wings and sang:

'Holy, holy, Lord God of Hosts, Prince of Peace, Ruler of the Heavenly Throng. There's none like him on earth!'

There were millions of quadrillions of angels and all of them had different colours on their wings. Some were purplish, others sky-blue, dark like the Two-tailed Pasha or light yellow like the Brimstone. It was a magnificent sight with all those pairs of wings fluttering and shimmering in the brilliance of the snow-white clouds. But even more beautiful was their singing and the music. No one could describe it. Angel voices are more beautiful than all human voices and musical instruments. It sounded more beautiful than Aunt Laura's singing to the guitar, more beautiful even than when we sing 'O, du seelige, o, du fröhliche . . .' on Christmas Eve, more beautiful than when Pappa plays Bach on Sunday mornings so that the whole room shakes and the score falls off the piano. Not even the Ninth, which Grandmother and Grandfather heard in Vienna, can be compared to it. And yet there were huge gentlemen there with voices as deep as out of a barrel and ladies who could zoom up to the top notes – violins, harps, clarinets and cocottes, trumpets and horrible contra-bassoons, all played so that you thought the roof would come off.

Of course it must have been terribly difficult to talk up there, because one person could scarcely hear what the other was saying. Actually, it's strange that God didn't get tired of it all. But Grandmother says that if something is sufficiently beautiful, you never get tired of it. The angels wished for nothing better than that God should be pleased with their singing, as he sat there enthroned on the very top of the highest cloud, surrounded by light in his chair between the four beasts.

At the time, Lucifer was an archangel. Gabriel, Raphael and Michael were his brothers. And God liked Lucifer best, because he was the most beautiful of all the angels. Lucifer used to lead the choir of angels. When the other angels stopped singing, a silvery clear voice rose out of the silence that at once fell over the shimmering snowy landscape of clouds. The heights were filled with its pure resonance as time stood still, and God and all the angels listening to the singing forgot everything else. God singled out Lucifer from all the other angels and fastened a diadem on his forehead, where a morning star flashed like a diamond.

But Lucifer's heart was filled with pride when he saw how honoured and loved he was and he wearied of praising the power and glory of God. One day he slipped away from the choir of angels without anyone noticing. He dived through the cloud cover and floated down into the dark depths opening out below him. As he flew across the silent waters, he saw his reflection appear out of the depths and float up towards him. And he saw his beauty and fell in love with his own image.

'Who is more beautiful than I am?' he said to himself, stroking the surface of the water lightly with his outspread wings, as if embracing his own image and almost touching it like a swallow before a storm. He couldn't see enough of himself.

'Why should I obey him?' he went on. 'Why should I sing all those songs of praise in his honour day in and day out? Am I not more beautiful, younger and more adorable than he? Have I not more right to be worshipped by the angels and to rule over the heights?'

Ever since that day, Lucifer visited the misty depths over and over again. They drew him down there, in solitude, silence, the eternal night, out of which his image rose surrounded by the light of the diadem of stars. He persuaded other angels to follow him down there. A great many of the angels were in love with him and allowed themselves to be seduced. They stopped praising God and slipped away from the choir without anyone finding out. They were frightened down there in the darkness and anxiously gathered round Lucifer, but Lucifer said they had nothing to fear. He praised their wisdom and courage, praised their beauty and let them mirror their features in the waves of the depths. Then he took each and every one of them into his embrace and pressed a kiss to their lips.

With this trick, Lucifer succeeded in seducing more and more angels. They forgot God and fell by the wayside. The throng that secretly stood at his side grew day by day. It went so far that even God began to think the celestial music was sounding a little thin and was not roaring through eternity with the same strength as before. 'I think I'm beginning to be hard of hearing,' he said to the archangels in a circle round his throne. 'But I suppose it's my age. Not even I can manage to count up how old I shall be this year.'

One day God was feeling rather tired and bored by the eternal concert and was dozing on his throne. So Lucifer summoned his faithful, flew off to a distant cloud and started singing. He sang so beautifully that one by one the choir of angels fell silent and listened entranced to his singing. But it was no hymn of praise to God but a hymn about the glory and greatness of Lucifer himself. And the song was so terrible and Lucifer so beautiful as he stood there on the edge of the cloud with his fiery-eyed wings outspread against the blue heights, the glowing jewel of the morning star on his forehead, the angels fell to their knees and worshipped him in place of God. He proclaimed himself Prince of the Heights, The Highest, He who Rules from Eternity to Eternity. Then off he flew at the head of his army to kill God and take over ruling the universe.

They were already quite close when God woke up from his afternoon nap, yawned, sat up on his throne, rubbed his eyes and looked around. In actual fact he had only been pretending to be asleep just to deceive Lucifer.

For God is all-knowing. He sees and hears everything. He knew all about Lucifer's outings down into the depths, his love of himself, his treachery and the conspiracy of the seduced angels – he even knew at that very moment how the struggle between himself and Lucifer would end, for God can see into the future as well. And yet it made the veins in his forehead swell and his face turn red as he trembled with fury. 'Treachery!' he roared, banging his fist on the arm of the throne so that the four beasts yelped with terror. 'Ha! Ah! Michael, Gabriel, Raphael! Don't stand there with your mouths open! Is that the way to do your guard duty? Can't I have a moment's peace without everything turning upside-down?'

There was general tumult as the angels threw away their zithers and violins and rushed hither and thither.

'Away with you, scoundrels!' roared God. 'Draw your swords and show the traitor what it means to raise his hand against his King and God: Michael, take command!'

The terrified Michael hastily summoned together all the angels still on the side of God and flew to confront Lucifer. His throng collided with the fallen angels and there was a terrible battle up there in heaven. The clash of weapons and the shrieks of the fighters echoed through the heights and depths. The sound was so thunderous, you would have thought the universe would fall apart, for there were millions of quadrillions of angels, seraphs, cherubs, djinns and spirit princes coming to blows. The battle rolled back and forth, but in the end Michael was victorious and Lucifer and all his adherents fell down into the depths. It must have been a sight when the cloud cover split apart, the heavenly light flashed through and lit up the misty depths! Quadrillions of fallen angels were floating down with shattered burning wings, flaring up and dying away like falling stars. Much later on, the heights were full of torn-off seraph wings and cherub feathers, fluttering hither and thither and rocking on the waves of those depths that had once mirrored Lucifer's features. It looked as if the water were strewn with dead butterflies. But one after the other, the feathers were sucked down into the depths, their colours fading and the water glimmering again, black and silent, as in a well.

In the morning, I wanted to know how Lucifer had got on, because I was feeling sorry for him. Had he drowned?

'Angels can't die,' said Grandmother. 'He was banished for ever from the brotherhood. His diadem was torn from his head, his seraph wings crushed in the fall against the rock. His supernatural beauty was transformed into the most forbidding ugliness. He became Satan, the Prince of Sin and Darkness.'

I carefully took the postcard off the desk to look closer at it. The back was covered with Satan's ugly spiky scrawl – perhaps it was an account of the events Grandmother had hinted at. The landscape must be the peak of the Fire Mountain near Salmela, though it was hard to recognize on that picture. Satan must have hit himself so terribly hard when he fell down on that rock. It's frightening to look at his face, his elbow, chest and his tense side. The only nice thing is the shimmering bed of feathers he's lying on. You would never have imagined he had had so many feathers in his wings. They fill the whole picture and cover the ground like a carpet as far as the eye can see. When you swing the card to and fro in front of the window, it flares up like gold, and Satan himself disappears, but individual feathers appear even more clearly with their rainbow shimmering eyes and fine gold rays. You realize how beautiful he must have been and how huge were the wings he boasted about.

But Grandmother wouldn't let me look my fill. She snatched the card out of my hand, put it back in the desk drawer and turned the key. 'It's a godless picture,' she said. 'It glorifies sin and damnation.'

UNCLE GEORG LIVES JUST BEHIND THE FALKENHEIMER aunts' veranda. The sun never shines on his window. It's shadowy there and cool and the dewdrops tremble in the leaves of the weeds in front of the stone base. A thermometer is fastened with an iron clamp to the window-frame and shines against the dark window-pane. It's the largest and most important thermometer here at Teerilä. Uncle Georg always looks at it before deciding whether he will let us freeze or sweat the next moment. Actually, he rules over the weather and it really is no easy matter keeping track of all the secret forces that go with that. He hardly has time to do anything else at all.

Every evening he has to go out to look at the sunset, and from the position of the sun, the colours of the clouds and the length of the shadows, he reads off the weather he is to prepare for the next day. He often stands with his watch in his hand looking intently at the sun, the dazzling edge of which is already brushing the tree-tops on the other side of the fields. He has to keep looking to see if the sun is keeping to the agreed time and really does set at the moment it's been told to. Not until the last glimpse of the sun flares up like a flame and goes out in among the spruce-tops does he click the watch-case shut and put his watch back into his waistcoat pocket.

Sometimes all has gone well, but at other times he is visibly annoyed. He stamps with impatience, pokes behind his ear with his pencil and draws a cross in his notebook.

He also keeps track of the clouds. He often walks round with his head thrown back, thrashing about with his stick and looking straight up at the sky so that you're afraid he'll fall flat in a puddle like Johnny Head-in-Air. But he doesn't do that to say something nice about the clouds, the heavens or the greatness of God, like the other grown-ups. On the contrary, he is seldom satisfied with what he sees up there. The clouds are hardly ever the shape, size or colour he would like them to be. Either they aren't there just when he's expecting them, or they gather in far too large clusters above his head. I once saw Uncle Georg threaten a ragged dragon-shaped cloud as it shot up over the edge of the forest. He and slim Uncle Erni were quarrelling dreadfully in front of the hay barn.

'Tjort vosmij!' shouted Uncle Erni. 'It's coming this way.'

'Yes, it's coming this way. I told you, but . . .'

'The wind's coming straight from that direction!' snapped Uncle Erni, pointing at the cloud.

'No!' Uncle Georg put his finger in his mouth and raised it menacingly up in front of the cloud. 'It's coming from over there. Damn it!' He raised his stick and pointed behind him. 'It's sailing against the wind!'

'Following wind, I say!'

'No, head wind.'

'Clouds move like this,' snapped Uncle Erni, angrily sweeping his hand across his line of vision.

'No, like this!' Uncle Georg's sweep was even angrier but went in the opposite direction.

'It's going to rain. The hay's got to be got in. . . . You . . .'

'But I say no!' growled Uncle Georg. 'It's against all the rules. The wind's pressing on and it won't work with the best will in the world.' He threw up his stick like a sword and lunged at the cloud. 'It'll go like this, then like that. Then that's the end. There won't be any rain.' He stamped his foot. 'I say no! No, no and no!'

Uncle Georg's expression and the fire that flared suddenly out of the raised ferrule really did stop that insolent dragon cloud. It crept along the edge of forest all afternoon, grumbling angrily and shooting its glistening humps up towards the base of the sky. But it didn't dare come and the thunderstorm Uncle Erni had predicted never materialized. In the end it thought it might as well obey orders and go the way Uncle Georg had staked out for it, slanting across the sky and disappearing behind Oravansaari. It sailed away in dark blue, white-edged fragments which grew more and more ragged and finally dissolved, the last remains melting away in a golden shower of rain above Salmela. Two rainbows – the one shimmering and clear and the other dull and almost invisible – were arching over there. We all went out into the garden to look at them. But when Uncle Georg strolled past, he just shook his head crossly. 'It's not good at all, Muscha! Not at all. That copper-coloured mist over there! Look at the way the birch twigs are hanging. A proper breeze should come along and blow the whole lot away.'

After his evening walk Uncle Georg retreats to his room, which he calls 'the office'. It's large and shadowy and full of peculiar metal and glass objects. A globe of the world stands on the desk between piles of papers and old books. The walls are covered with maps and large squared placards, on which he draws scrolls and crosses with a red and a blue pen. There's a map of the whole sky there, too, and on it even the smallest star is a white dot. He knows the names of every single one of them and can point out the Bull, Gemini, the Great Bear and the Little Bear and other peculiar star creatures on the map, although I have never managed to see anything except the same muddle of white dots under the fingernail of his forefinger.

His light is still on late at night. When night has come and everyone else is asleep, he's still sitting in there, leaning over his desk, his penholder in his mouth, leafing through heaps of paper and thinking about the weather he's preparing for the next day. Sometimes he puts the pen down, gets up with his hands propped on the desk top and looks up at the stars watching his tireless labours through the window. I presume Uncle Georg sleeps even less than Grandmother, and she doesn't really sleep at all. He has to get up even before sunrise to look at the thermometer, examine the mists out on the fields, taste the dewdrops in the garden and, watch in hand, wait up by the stables for the sun.

When we come round the corner of his house in the mornings, he calls over from the woodshed and comes across to us with the axe in his hand. 'There was a frost last night!' he says breathlessly. 'Below zero at three o'clock. One and a half degrees Celsius!'

The most important thing in Uncle Georg's room is the barometer, a peculiar wooden-framed glass thing-ummy with shiny brass things inside. It mostly looks like a wall-clock. Uncle Georg is terribly careful of it and once smacked my fingers when I reached out to touch it. He can never decide what the weather's going to be like until he has put his glasses on and stood tugging at his beard in front of the barometer for a while. Sometimes he taps on the barometer glass. It tinkles and the needle jerks. He clears his throat, chews on his moustache, turns the knob on the barometer, takes the red pen off his desk and goes and stands in front of the squared placard.

If anyone asks him what the weather's going to be like, he hardly ever gives a straight clear answer. 'Changeable, Anni,' he grunts, shrugging his shoulders. 'Changeable. I can't yet say anything more. . . .'

But sometimes he knows at once. His face goes dark red and his fingers shake as he turns the needle back to its place. Puffing and panting, he rushes over to the placard, sweeps the pen across it and throws the pen down with a curse and heads for the stand where his oilskin hangs. 'Storm! Bad weather!' he rumbles, clumping down the steps. Sometimes, when we're on our way to the shore to go out rowing, he appears in front of us like some strange sea monster, enveloped in his crinkly oilskin coat, his white beard glistening under the hood. 'Back!' he thunders, lifting his leather mitten like a fin. 'Back! Going rowing? Ridiculous! Ho ho. The barometer says stormy.'

For a moment he stays there staring at us with his cloudy old eyes. His chest goes up and down, the soft whiskers round his lips flap and the grey in those eyes of his gets darker as if the shadows of the clouds were sweeping through them. You can feel the storm already raging inside him and he has to strain his whole will to stop it breaking out and sweeping over Teerilä before all the precautionary measures have been taken. With an incomprehensible bellow, he leaves us and rushes away over to the Big House balcony.

'Bad weather. Storm!' he roars, striking the wooden railings with his knobbly stick so that the white paint flakes off and flies all over the place. 'Else! Leli! Can't you hear? Are you mad, leaving the washing hanging out here? Is it to fly off into the forest or be washed into the sea by the cloudburst?'

Terrified faces appear in the windows. One of the aunts rushes down the steps and over to the washing-line tied between the oaks and starts taking down the washing. The garments flap and flutter round her like a flock of frightened geese. Uncle Frans's silvery mane and square-cut beard put in an appearance above the railing he's been resting behind on a deck-chair.

'Ho! Ho! Frans!' rumbles Uncle Georg. 'A herher Storm! A herher Hurricane! Tout à fait! Voilà! Blidda! Blidda!'

While we're still standing on the same spot where he'd stopped us, squabbling over whether we should really have to go back or go on, he sweeps by with his pointed hood askew over one eye and his oilskin crackling round him.

'Scandalous! The hay! Erni! Have you seen Erni?'

Without waiting for Grandmother to answer, he turns aside: 'The windows! Shut the windows! And close the shutters! The telephone. Ho ho. The telephone! Disconnect it!'

He waves his knobbly stick at the aunt who is still struggling with the washing under the oaks and sails away over towards the fields where workers and old women are moving among the haycocks like brightly coloured little toy figures.

Sometimes the storm Uncle has conjured up breaks over Teerilä more quickly than you could ever have imagined. His shouts are followed by a menacing rumble over from the forest. Dark clouds gather in the sky and the oaks rustle. Dust and dead nasturtium leaves swirl up from the road and the rain pours down before we've had time to get to our steps. But the storm is more often long in coming.

The sky is still blue, the sun blazing down and everything looks so peaceful, the Grown-ups decide on the boat trip after all. Later on, as we splash our way home through the puddles and streams of water, our clothes dripping and crumpled, he stands in front of his steps roaring with laughter, beaming under his rain hood, his oilskin glistening as if it were lacquered and water pouring down through its folds in dark rivulets. 'Soaked!' he cries. 'Like drowned rats! Ho ho. What did I tell you! That'll give you something to think about.'

But sometimes the outing has exceeded all expecta-tions as, tired and sweaty, we trail past the corner of Uncle Georg's house. Then he pretends not to see us and stays over by the woodshed, chopping wood. When Grandmother is with us, she can't resist stopping and calling out to him: 'A wonderful outing, Georg! Perfect weather, I must say.'

Uncle Georg rubs his forearm across his forehead and slowly rolls up the shirt-sleeve that has come down. 'The storm,' he says gloomily. 'It'll come all right. You'll see, Muscha.'

'When?' says Grandmother. 'Tomorrow or perhaps next month? I can hardly wait.'

Uncle Georg doesn't answer. He takes a log and props it upright on the chopping-block. 'Damn you!' he snorts when the log falls over. 'Stand up! Stand up, I say, you bugger!'

He grasps the axe with both hands and brings it down with a crash. The log splits with a hoarse croak, chips and bark fly around and one half of the log comes whirling over towards us like a bowled-over skittle.

Sometimes the storm breaks just as Grandmother says, days or even weeks later than Uncle Georg has announced. Sometimes I think it completely fails to appear and the showers are often so short and slight it sounds like an empty boast when Uncle Georg calls them storms and makes such a fuss about them. So I've a feeling that the sun, the clouds, the winds and everything else to do with the weather don't obey Uncle Georg nearly so much as he likes to make out. Often the weather does exactly the opposite of what he wants. Then he gets bad-tempered and shouts and bellows as soon as anyone even mentions the weather. Several of the Grown-ups maintain it is always the opposite of what Uncle Georg has said: if he forecasts rain, you know it'll be fine weather, and if he talks about a thaw, there's sure to be a frost. Grandmother says God's the only one to decide on the weather and anyone trying to forecast the weather is putting himself above God. His human understanding will always get the worst of it.

I'm not sure Grandmother is right, because of course that's how Grandmother would like it to be, because the will of God and Grandmother's will are really one and the same. I suspect Grandmother secretly muddles the weather up for Uncle Georg because she envies his power over the winds and the clouds.

ONE DAY BERNT AND I HAD INVESTIGATED A DITCH
over by the Vendelä road. A tangle of burdock leaves and
hogweed filled the ditch and, when you got into it, you
fell right through all that greenery down into a deep hole.
A secretive green half-light reigned down at the bottom,
and the burdock leaves made a kind of roof over your
head in which small transparent snails had gnawed holes
here and there. It was cramped and stuffy, the stiff stalks
prickling your elbows and knees, and small coin-shaped
patches of sunlight danced on your hands and lit up the
dead grass stalks and white threads of roots underneath
you. It was fun sitting down there as if in a tent, listening
to the bees and flies singing up above and hearing a crow
cawing and a cart rattling past and knowing you were
quite invisible to everyone.

We cut flutes with Bernt's penknife out of the stems
of the hogweed. You couldn't blow through them at first,
because at the joints the stalks were blocked by white
sugary stuff you had to poke out with the tip of the knife,
but then the stalks made fine green pipes and we blew
through them into each other's faces so that it tickled
and you had to screw up your eyes. Bernt cut a pipe
for himself that whistled when he blew through it. But
I didn't succeed in doing the same, although I blew my
cheeks out and strained so much everything went black
before my eyes. Then I thought it just as well to sing
through the pipe, which really sounded more beautiful,
and the singing had a strange muffled resonance as if
an elephant were trumpeting through his trunk. Bernt

said that if we played for long enough, the snakes would crawl out of their holes and dance for us. There must have been snakes listening to us somewhere nearby, because the ditch was quite near the bench where Aunt Dulla had once seen a grass snake. But the grass snake didn't come out although we played until our lips were sore and our ears popping, and I just caught a glimpse of his gold-spotted head several times in among the stalks.

After a while we set off home. Bernt said it was getting on and we had to run so as not to be late for dinner. We took the shortest route, through the elder and bird-cherry bushes below big Aunt Lala's house and then taking a short cut across the meadow.

Kaima was standing in our way. It felt rather awful going so close to him. You never knew what he might do when he caught sight of us. To my surprise, he neither moved nor turned his head as we crept past his tall dark hindquarters and his whisking tail. I wondered whether he'd even noticed us. Then I suddenly saw something terribly peculiar. Something long and black hung down between Kaima's hind legs. I showed Bernt, but he didn't know what it was either. We turned round and went closer to be able to see better. But Kaima turned away, lashing out at us with his tail-whisk and trotting off slowly with the black thing dangling and swinging round his legs. He stopped a little way away from us, his hindquarters turned towards us, and covered himself with his tail so we couldn't see anything. He was clearly annoyed that we had surprised him, and didn't want us to see anything more. But we didn't leave him alone. We went after him, ignoring the angry tossing of his head, his glaring eyes and impatient snorts. In the end we managed to catch up with him so that we could see him from the side. A strange sort of rod really was sticking out of his belly. It was terribly long and big and swung heavily, as if made of rubber.

As soon as we got home, we told Grandmother and Mamma what we'd seen. Grandmother walked up and down the room, stick in hand, pursing her lips and looking at us for a long time without saying anything. I could see from her eyes that she was cross, but for some reason she didn't want us to notice.

'This . . .' she said in the end. 'This is truly extraordinary. I simply can't understand how you could have seen such a thing.'

'But it's true!' we protested. 'We saw it. We're not making it up.'

'Then,' said Grandmother, most displeased, 'then you saw something that children never usually see.'

'But what was it?' we persisted.

Grandmother exchanged a swift glance with Mamma. 'Then it must have been . . . I can't think of anything except. . . .' She clamped her lips together and cleared her throat. 'It must have been the horse's intestine,' she said finally, jabbing the floor with her stick.

'Yes,' said Mamma, her face red. 'What's so special about that? Why shouldn't a horse occasionally let his intestine out to air it?'

'Anyhow,' Grandmother went on, looking sternly at us, 'intestines are nasty and dirty. Nasty and dirty!' she repeated, banging her stick on the floor. 'Nice children turn away from things like that and try to cover their eyes. Sins get in through the eye very easily and soil the soul.'

'One doesn't usually', added Mamma, 'stand looking on when other people see to their needs. It's just the same for animals as it is for human beings. When an animal does things like that, you go away or look the other way.'

'But Kaima wasn't peeing at all, or doing his big business,' I tried explaining to Mamma.

'Don't argue,' she snapped. 'There's no great difference in what one does when it's a matter of those parts of the body. One shouldn't be inquisitive about dirty things. And one doesn't talk about such things either, or think about them.'

Grandmother raised her forefinger and added: 'Ye shall not make yourselves abominable with any creeping thing that creepeth, neither shall ye make yourselves unclean with them, that ye should be defiled thereby. For I am the Lord your God.'

'Now go out and play,' said Mamma, pushing us through the door. 'And don't think about this any longer. Go and tell Aunt to come here. We have to talk to her.'

JUST AS I AM ABOUT TO PUT JACKO MY MONKEY TO bed and am putting on his pale blue flannel jerkin, I hear the first cowbell. The bells are still clanging, distant and dreamlike right inside the dark forest. You can hear them for a moment whenever the birds stop chattering in the garden. They're in such a hurry to call good-night to each other, they make a terrible racket before they fall asleep.

But after a while the bells sound quite clear and close. I throw Jacko aside so that he lies on the floor with his jerkin unbuttoned and his hairy arms stretched up in a helpless and reproachful gesture. I can still see nothing from the window, only Hämäläinen and Ali walking past with their scythes on their shoulders and Kuri Mari in her black kerchief and her yellow and red striped apron. She's holding a disobedient cockerel clamped under her arm. The cockerel is kicking angrily and twisting his head about, but Kuri Mari takes no notice at all, just carries him home to say her prayers with him and put him to bed.

Then there are more and more bells, the clanging now coming from every direction, as if invisible creatures were roaming through our garden and slipping round the house. The clanging is mixed with the tramp of cloven hoofs and a woman's singing voice calling urgently:

'Tuulikki, Tuulikki, tuu, come, come,
Tuulikki, Tuulikki, tuu, come, come!'

After a little while the heads of the leading cows appear over the top of the hill where the road curves.

37

The sun flaring over the edge of the forest is dazzling and the cows look like black shadows, only their backs and horns glowing as if gilded and the dust round them shining as though the cows themselves were radiating a secretive shimmer.

I rush off into the kitchen and press my face to the window. Now I can see the cows quite close. There's a terrible noise going on out there. They're tolling their bells as hard as they can, some of them tossing their heads and bellowing wildly, cows of all kinds, brown all over, cocoa-coloured with a white star on their foreheads, all white with great sorrowful eyes and gentle humble looks, black and white patterned ones and colourful ones with a touch of blue here and there. The colourful cows look like Indians in war-paint. One of them looks particularly menacing, because she's gored off one of her horns and the other horn is bent like a crooked nail down towards her muzzle. One at a time the cows trot past in an endless line, so many of them it's impossible to count them, perhaps fifty, perhaps a hundred, perhaps a thousand, most of them trotting along with lowered horns and necks stretched out, not looking round. Their udders swing like great bags between their hind legs.

Then one large cow blocks the others' way. She tugs at tufts of grass on the roadside and starts quite leisurely grazing the hedge Pappa has planted round the kitchen garden. The other cows, which can't get by, make their way off the road and some of them look as if they're going to come into us. One young heifer with small budlike teats goes up to the kitchen steps, sniffs at the railing, lifts her tail like a pigtail and drops a cowpat. But Anna comes rushing out and gives her a smart rap on the back so that she sets off with clumsy bounds like a fat rabbit, stumbling over the mossy stones.

At once all the cows set off at a bound, bells clanging and udders bouncing, as if fleeing. At that moment I catch sight of Bull. He's striding along quite calmly and unmoved. His head is quite black with a moonlike white patch on his forehead and there's a shiny gold ring in his nose. His body is all irregular black and white patches, as if he were tattooed. He resembles the cows, but is in every way larger and more awful, so I recognize him straight away. His head is heavier, his forehead broader and his shoulders arch menacingly over the short thick neck. Between his forelegs, his brisket hangs in a loose fold which is swinging from side to side. His trunk, which comes next, is as long and high up as the boiler on a steam-engine. Under his belly dangles a dirty tuft of hair and between his hind legs swings a pale pink thing that reminds you of the clapper on a church bell.

'Bull!' I cry to Kirsti, who is over by the stove. 'Bull's coming.'

But Kirsti doesn't want to look. When I turn back again, Bull gives me such a stern look out of his belligerent white eye that I hastily retreat from the window.

I daren't stay outside when the cows go past. They usually push their way into our grounds, sniffing quite blatantly at my toys that have been left on the sandy path and munching away at some flower in the flower-bed until Kirsti or one of the farm girls manages to chase them off. They also bellow so angrily and loudly when they see me, I jump and drop my spade in the sand. These giants, with their barrel-like bodies, glaring eyes and terrifying horns, would surely tear me to pieces if I dared go too close to them. And yet it isn't the cows that make me so careful. For even if they are sometimes nasty and frighten me by shaking their heads and bellowing, I still know they like me. The milk I drink every morning and evening is the pledge of a secret alliance between us.

It's Bull I'm afraid of. He doesn't give any milk and even the Grown-ups are afraid of him, so carefully get out of the way when they come across him. Only the farm girls and the cowman dare go near him, and even them he treats as he pleases. He has gored out Riika's eye so all she's got left there is a staring blood-red hole and she goes around peering, her face all crooked. He took Pekkala the cowman on his horns, tossed him into the air and broke his spine. Pekkala is in hospital now and they've had to get another cowman. It's a miracle Bull contented himself with just breaking his spine and didn't tear him apart like an earthworm. No one has dared punish Bull for these wicked deeds – even Grandmother is afraid to go out into the garden when he comes past. The only thing they've dared do is to fasten a gold ring in his nose as a sign of his wickedness. It gives him an even more bloodthirsty appearance, so he looks like a real man-eater. But he's not at all ashamed of that ugly ring. On the contrary, he seems to be proud of it and regards it as an ornament, a sign of royal dignity they've given him out of fear and subservience.

But the most awful thing about him is still not that he's Bull. The awful thing is that he's also Baal or Beel, the idol who has kept up a feud with God since the beginning of time. He's the one Grandmother means when she teaches us the first commandment: Thou shalt have no other gods before me for I am the Lord thy God.

For from the very first moment, Baal has demanded that people shall worship him instead of God and has seduced them into worshipping graven images. As early as just after the Deluge, he managed to get people to desert God. That became such an abomination, Grandmother says, that she had to leave the country of Uri together with Abraham and Lot, in order to avoid being part of it any longer. And when they went past the towns of Sodom and Gomorrah, Baal had tempted the people there to sin so dreadfully that God was forced to drown both towns in a shower of fire and burning sulphur. When Moses then wandered through the desert for forty years with the children of Israel, Baal kept seducing the children into being disobedient and grumbling at God. While Moses was sitting up on Mount Sinai in a thunder-cloud, talking to God, the children started grumbling about the good semolina God rained down from the sky, and longing for the stew-pots of Egypt. When Grandmother couldn't get any meat, they made an idol of Baal's son, the Golden Calf.

Grandmother's voice shakes with annoyance at this disobedience. Her eyes get a distant look in them and she raises her hand in a dismissive gesture. It's just as if she were seeing it in front of her all over again. And when I follow Grandmother's gaze, which is fixed on the wall opposite, I can see the wall glide aside and the desert landscape appear from behind. We both see the way the children garland themselves, put gold rings on their arms and then hand in hand whirl round the Golden Calf. Their purple Sunday-best clothes flap like flags and their bodies are exposed in an immodest way. It's bad enough that their best clothes are completely ruined, but that's a minor matter compared with the awful sin they commit as they dance like that and worship the calf.

It's not surprising Moses was cross and smashed the tablets on which God had inscribed the ten commandments with so much labour. Though Grandmother probably thinks he went too far and frightened the children too much. She tried to dissuade him in every way from doing it. But, although the Golden Calf was ground into sand and the children were beaten, which they certainly deserved, their love for the idol never ceased except for a short time. However much Moses, Grandmother and other God-fearing people warned them, the children were never satisfied. They constantly fussed about the semolina pudding, grumbled at Moses and degenerated into idol worship. Despite the terrible punishment they had to endure – when the serpents came wriggling in the desert sand, when they were attacked by Amalekites, Ammonites and Trilobites – they had no desire to improve.

Things went on like this even later on. King Ahab and the wicked Queen Jezebel built a magnificent idol temple to Baal, where he was worshipped and served day and night by hundreds of priests. Elijah scolded Jezebel and warned her and said that if she went on with this abomination she would fall out of the palace window and be eaten up by dogs. But Jezebel just laughed and ordered the soldiers to seize Elijah and throw him into prison, so Elijah had to flee far away to a desolate mountain where no one could find him.

Elijah lay there sleeping behind a big rock and was fed by a raven God sent down to him. The raven came flying down with an egg-shaped wheaten bun in its beak and laid it carefully on the flat stone beside him. Elijah slept all the while. Sometimes he moved in his sleep and his stomach rumbled. Not until the raven flew away did he sit up, rub his eyes and call out with delight for Grandmother to show her the freshly baked bun. When they had shared it, he turned over on his side, sighing with contentment, then fell asleep again.

For seven years they lived like this, far away from people on this desolate mountain, while Baal ruled over the whole country and Jezebel and the other idol worshippers thought he had died long ago. But as the years went by, God ordered them to rise and go to Ahab's palace. Elijah promised to do conjuring tricks to show that God was mightier than Baal. But Ahab and Jezebel just smiled, so certain were they that the Baal priests were better conjurors than Elijah.

It was an abomination to see this spectacle going on hour after hour. The priests' faces and bared chests were criss-crossed with deep cuts oozing blood. The little pointed sacrificial knives in their hands glinted and ripped up arms, hips and thighs like the flesh of fruit. They wailed, rocking back and forth, and the mirror-bright marble floor in front of the idol was spattered with blood as if the temple were a slaughterhouse. But nothing happened. The sacrificial wood did not catch alight and, however much Ahab and Jezebel searched and peered with their hands shielding their eyes in the burning sunlight, not the tiniest little cloud appeared in the sky.

In the end Grandmother couldn't control herself and urged Elijah to appear. And Grandmother had never before experienced a thunderstorm banging and crashing and the lightning flashing like the one Elijah conjured forth. While the sacrificial fire on Elijah's altar crackled like a midsummer bonfire and the water poured down so that it turned as dark as night, the people rushed around, tripping over each other and yelling for the umbrellas they had forgotten to take with them. Later on, Ahab sat weeping like a little child. He begged and implored Elijah to forgive him and ordered all the priests of Baal to be executed. On that occasion Baal had to admit defeat and hand over his place to God the Father, who is the only true and almighty god and therefore he alone has the right to all honour.

But Baal didn't give up. Time and again he came back and occasionally it looked as if he had been victorious over God for ever. And somehow you can understand people preferring to worship Baal rather than God and preferring to obey him. For Baal is in every way much more horrible than God and so, of course, people fear him more.

God is like a nice old uncle with a big white beard like Uncle Frans. He mostly flies around in a night-shirt or with large flapping sheets wound round his body. Sometimes he looks stern, but generally his face is kind and friendly, so you quite forget he can conjure much worse and more quickly than anyone else. It's difficult to have any kind of idea of his size, because he seems to change as he pleases. Sometimes he's gigantic, so the edges of his cloak embrace the whole canopy of the sky, but he usually seems to be no bigger than Uncle Frans or Uncle Georg – in fact a little smaller.

On the other hand, Baal is as big as a house. He's got a bull's head and large protruding, glowing white eyes. His mouth smiles cruelly and frighteningly, as if he were looking in on himself and was delighted about something only he knows about. The smile hides his face like a mask. His nostrils tremble as he hungrily sniffs at the air. He seems to be constantly drawing into himself the sacrificial smoke rising up to him. His body is as high as a tower and made of polished blocks of granite piled on top of each other. Stiffly upright, his back straight, he sits on his throne with his knees together, his arms down his sides. In that position, without moving, he receives people's homage as they kneel in front of his throne, raising their hands and begging for mercy.

Right in the middle of his stomach, just below his waist, is a square gaping hole that reminds you of a furnace door, everything inside red and glowing. The flames lick his belly, wisps of smoke curl round his head and the whole terrifying figure trembles slightly in the red glow, lighting it up from below. People approach timidly with little children in their raised hands. They fall to their knees in front of Baal's throne and then throw the children's naked bodies in through the glowing red furnace door.

It's terrible to see and terrible to think that parents could do such a thing with their children. But you have only to raise your eyes to Baal's rigidly smiling face to feel that you have to obey, and you yourself also feel the desire to do so. His belly is insatiable. The fire inside never goes out. The more children thrown in through the door, the more satisfied his smile becomes. He seems to be silently counting the children slaughtered and sacrificed to him. Sometimes he can't control his impatience. He snatches the child's body out of the kneeling mother's hands, tears it apart with his claws, bites off its head and gobbles it up bit by bit. Flames and smoke swirl up out of his mouth and nostrils and his hands are smeared with blood.

Sometimes he's not content with just children — youths and maidens are slaughtered and their helplessly exposed slack bodies are dragged up and handed over to him. When he has wearied of human flesh, whole bodies of animals, stallions and oxen are hurled down into his belly. Then he may drop his mask for a moment and show his delight in a series of monkey-like leaps. He slaps his thighs and the temple echoes with his bellows and peals of laughter.

People don't shower Baal with these sacrificial offerings just because they are so afraid of him. The sacrifices are also a kind of barter. When the parents kill their children and hand them over to the idol, they get something in return, something that pleases them. After that he protects and defends them and they become participants in his power, as if they themselves had become little idols.

Bernt has a book about Hannibal, whom Baal made into a great hero. I'm allowed to look at the pictures sometimes. Hannibal was only nine when he swore to the enthroned Baal he would take revenge on the Romans because they had maltreated his father. The dark-haired boy in a short-sleeved tunic looks like a girl, but the gesture he is making with his upstretched arm is commanding and passionate. His father is standing behind him, fully equipped for war, and he has his hand protectively on his son's shoulder. In the background you can just see Baal's horned head, listening to the boy's oath with a satisfied and cruel smile. No wonder the Romans lost their heads when Hannibal had grown up and, at the head of an army of warriors and elephants, he marched into their country in order, with Baal's assistance, to demand revenge. That oath must have had terrible strength.

Anyway, Baal's power has become weaker and weaker recently. You could say he's already seriously heading for his fall and the final collapse is nigh. He's clearly subordinate to God nowadays. No temples are built any more in his honour and no priests serve him as they did in the past. He now lives his life in the shape of an old bull in the darkness of the byre in the dung and straw. But at night he still receives praise and sacrifices from people. That happens in the greatest of secrecy in a place no one knows.

Grandmother's voice trembles with her confidence in victory as she adjusts her spectacles and reads:

'Bel boweth down, Nebo stoopeth, their idols were upon the beasts, and upon the cattle: your carriages were heavy loaden; they are a burden to the weary beast. They stoop, they bow down together; they could not deliver the burden, but themselves are gone into captivity.'

ONE MORNING BAAL-BULL APPEARED ALL ALONE IN
the meadow in front of the nursery window, without his
usual following of submissive cows. After that he spent
long periods in the enclosure and the cows went past our
house every morning and evening without him.

When Tommy and I wanted to go out, we didn't want
to do what our aunt nurse told us and take our buckets
and spades down to the place where we usually played,
a flat smooth rock near the fence. Aunt assured us we
needn't be frightened and the fence would hold all right,
so Bull would never get out. But she strictly forbade us to
tease him and promised she would keep a look-out from
the window.

As we squatted on the big smooth stone and made
sand pies with our hands, Bull jogged back and forth,
sniffing and snorting at the bottom of the fence and
rubbing his chin on the top bar as if he were occasionally
overcome by an insufferable itch. It was rather horrid
seeing him so close, especially when he lowered his head
and rubbed his horn against the fence as if to test out his
strength. But it really did seem to hold. After making a
fuss for a while, he straightened up again and let out
a couple of rumbling bellows that made us jump and
cautiously retreat from the stone, at which he lolloped
away out into the meadow, contemptuously swinging his
tail.

In time we got used to the tramp of Bull's heavy
cloven hoofs, his angry snorts and nasty glaring looks,
and we scarcely looked up from our toys when he came

closer. For hours on end he would lie far away out on the meadow absently chewing on something, and the crunching sound of his teeth could be heard all the way to where we were playing. Sometimes he stood quite close behind the fence, breathing heavily and staring inquisitively, as if he didn't want to miss a single word we said or movement we made. It felt rather horrid and irritating and made us stop playing.

Once, when he had again stood staring like that for a long time, he suddenly stretched out his muzzle and let out a long-drawn-out hissing noise, as if wanting to blow us off that flat stone and urging us to go in search of another place to play in as soon as possible. Then he turned his head away, stretched out his hind legs and peed a vast pool on to the grass. It rushed out like a waterfall and the grass and flowers underneath him were covered with a white foam. I would never have imagined you could pee so much. I quite forgot Aunt's warning and decided to tease him. I showed Tommy Bull's two willies, which had long been bothering me, and we both laughed. It actually was rather funny that anyone could have two and they were also so unlike each other in shape and colouring. The tuft of hair on the front one, which he was using on that occasion, looked rather dirty and yellowish, like the crotch of your underpants when you happened to have peed in your pants but kept it secret.

When Bull almost at once responded to our laughter with an angry toss of his head and annoyed snorts, we were delighted. We leapt about on the smooth flat rock, pointing at his stomach and trying to imitate the rushing noise he made when he peed. The insult was clearly too much for him. He lowered his head and started tearing up the grass with his front hoofs so that lumps of earth and tussocks of grass flew all over the place. Then he drove his horn into the fence and heaved with all his might. He looked awful, his nostrils glowing, green slime welling out of his mouth and his eyes popping as if about to burst out of their sockets with rage. When the fence suddenly creaked, we grabbed each other by the hand and rushed off to the veranda. I thought we would never get there in time. Everything went black before our eyes and we thought the next moment we would fall over and give up the ghost out of terror.

I didn't dare turn round until we reached the nursery. I was so sure Bull had followed us and the next moment I would hear him rushing up the steps to bang on the veranda door.

'You haven't been teasing Bull, have you?' said Aunt, her face a little redder than usual.

We assured her of our innocence, and as no steps could be heard and all was quiet, my heart at last stopped thumping. When I went over to the window, I saw that the fence was quite whole and Bull hadn't managed to get out. He was galloping far away in the meadow with his horns down and tail in the air as if chasing an invisible enemy.

Everything would have been all right if that evening Aunt hadn't told me to go and fetch the toys we had forgotten on the stone when we had run away from Bull. When all my feeble excuses and attempts to palm off the assignment on to Tommy failed, and Aunt stubbornly stuck to her demand and kept talking about duty and obedience, I grew angry and threw myself screaming on to the floor. This led to her smacking my bottom and my becoming even more unreasonable. After yelling for a while – I was screaming at the top of my voice so that Bull must have heard and really enjoyed himself – I was seized by the shoulders and shaken so that my head almost came off. In the end I had to admit that I was afraid of Bull.

'Afraid of Bull!' repeated Aunt contemptuously. 'And you want to be a man!'

Aunt took me by the hand and dragged me out. I knew it was no use resisting any longer, because when she looked like that she might well tear you to pieces or do something even more awful. Nevertheless, I did feel safer and happier in mind in her company. I tried to wipe away my tears and snot with my free hand and tidy myself up as best I could so that Bull wouldn't have the pleasure of seeing me crying.

It was already chilly outside. The forest was dark and awful and a light mist was hovering over the meadow. Bull was lying far out in the meadow, his head turned away, as if he were deep in thought, veils of mist swirling thickest in the very place where he was lying. He was blowing them across the meadow to hide himself so that in the end the whole meadow and he himself would disappear into this milky bluish fog.

I was rather annoyed with Aunt for carelessly letting the spade rattle in the bucket, but Bull didn't turn his head once, as if he hadn't even noticed us. He was lying absolutely still and went on blowing mist through his nostrils. Although it looked as if we'd outwitted him, I couldn't help feeling he was only pretending. He'd heard every word of the scene and was waiting for us to come. He was averting his head now so that I shouldn't notice he was observing us.

When I woke in the morning I was no longer afraid of Bull. I thought it terribly funny we had dared to tease him and that he had looked rather foolish and silly when he got angry with us. When I reminded Tommy about the way Bull had behaved, he also burst out laughing.

We closed the nursery door so the Grown-ups wouldn't hear us playing that I was Bull. Tommy teased me when I peed. I peed so much that the whole of the nursery was flooded and our terrified toys were struggling in the waves, shouting for help. In the end, Tommy's teddy bear was drowned and the chairs and our chest of toys were all under water. We had to seek refuge on the table.

'Teddy wasn't drowned,' said Tommy crossly. 'You're talking rubbish. You're lying.'

'Of course he was drowned. Can't you see? He's fallen under the stool and the water's risen up to the door-handle. And I'm peeing even more.'

'Then Grandmother will come and cut it off,' said Tommy. He jumped down from the table to go and fetch the scissors from the chest. 'I'm Grandmother. Snip snap!'

'That won't help. Bull has two. And I'm peeing with the fat one. Even more's coming.'

At that moment the door opened and Grandmother came in. She never even noticed she was swamped in pee and that the pee was rushing out into the other room like a waterfall. Terrified, we fell silent.

Grandmother's face was stern and grave, but you couldn't tell whether she had noticed anything as she came in. She told us to get down off the table and tidy up after us. She went across to the window and looked thoughtfully out across at the forest, then adjusted the black lace cap she was wearing and pattered off out of the room.

After dinner, we were all sitting out on the veranda and the Grown-ups were waiting for coffee. Everything was calm and peaceful. Aunt brought in a fresh bilberry flan. After the Grown-ups had helped themselves, Mamma said we could have a piece each, because we'd been good and obedient all morning and played on our own in the nursery without making a fuss.

I already had my hand out to the dish Aunt was offering me, the piece of flan waiting, grains of sugar glittering on the blue-black preserve. But at that very moment Bull bellowed out there like a clap of thunder over the whole world, the windows rattled and he just wouldn't stop, but bellowed even louder. Even Grandmother put down her cup of coffee and said: 'What's the matter with Bull today?'

They all turned their heads and some of them went over to the window to look out.

'He's not ill, is he?' said someone, with a shake of the head. 'Perhaps we ought to inform Uncle Georg.'

'Come on, help yourself properly,' said Aunt impatiently. 'Why are you dawdling?'

Without looking any closer, I grabbed a piece, put it on my plate and jumped off my chair. What I saw as I propped my chin on the window-sill and peered out confirmed my very worst fears.

Bull was standing just below the veranda behind the fence. His back was arched, his tail stretched straight out behind him, his nose raised, and he was bellowing as if he wished to burst the very vault of the sky. His gigantic stomach was working like a pair of bellows. He was catching his breath, his voice breaking and now and again becoming a hoarse whistling. What frightened me most of all was the sight of his huge belly expanding and contracting so that his hip-bones and ribs appeared rhythmically under the skin and kept expelling chasm-like roars through his mouth.

Cautiously, I crept away from the window. Everyone was looking strangely at me, just as if they realized Bull meant me with his roars but were pretending they didn't. I didn't dare take the piece of flan – it was as if I had no right to it. Empty-handed, I ran into the nursery and shut the door. In there I crouched down in a corner while the roaring of Bull went on echoing outside with greater and greater fury, calling on heaven and earth as witness to the indignity he had suffered.

I don't know if Uncle Georg was summoned and managed to calm him down sufficiently so that for the moment he abandoned his plans for vengeance. Anyhow, the bellows ceased after a while and were replaced by an oppressive silence, which seemed ominous but at least indicated that the danger had been averted for the time being.

AS FAR AS I REMEMBER, IT WASN'T UNTIL A FEW days later that the dreadful thing happened.

We had managed to avoid playing on the dangerous flat stone. Perhaps Aunt stopped bothering to send us there when she saw that I was afraid of Bull. Instead we played in the garden on the other side of the house, where you couldn't see the meadow and Bull couldn't see us.

I was just about to put some homeless ants into a hollow with a roof of sticks across it, when a warning cry rang through the garden.

'Bull's loose!'

I hardly had time to look up and grasp what it was all about before I heard a huge crash and saw Bull charging out of the bushes running round the sunny side of the garden. He was only about ten or so strides away from me. I don't remember what happened next or how it happened, but I suddenly found myself in the safety of the veranda.

There was a terrible uproar. Everyone flung down their handwork and newspapers and fled with terrified shrieks to the back of the house. Petrified faces appeared in the windows. Bull was raging like a berserk in the garden. He leapt straight into Grandmother's yellow rose bush, smashing the branches like matchsticks, then uprooting the bank of flowers in the middle of the lawn with his hoofs. Chunks of earth and torn-off peonies and poppies were flung high up into the air, then finally he charged at Grandmother's basket chair, tipped it over with his horn and tore apart her black mantilla with his

53

front hoofs and one horn. It was dirty white and pointed and I could feel it boring into my stomach every time he twisted outwards and jerked at the mantilla.

'Oh, Bull!' said Grandmother, who had come out on to the veranda and had stood watching the destruction for a while. 'Oh, Bull! Why are you so angry? Why are you smashing my lovely flowers? Why are you wrecking my flower-beds? Why are you knocking over my basket chair and tearing holes in my mantilla?'

Bull snorted so that sand swirled up from the garden path, then he reared and butted the chair so that it spun off and landed far away in the ruined rose bush.

'I know no one as strong as you,' said Grandmother, crossing her hands over the ivory top of her walking-stick. 'Everyone fears you. But what have I done to you to make you rage against me and my flowers like this?'

Bull answered with a furious bellow. The ground shook like a clap of thunder and there was a flash like lightning. Even Grandmother's face jerked back as if from a blow. Bull rolled his eyes, lowered his head, thrust out his chin as if about to rub it against the ground and start crawling on all fours. The sight of his pinkish tongue thrust out of his mouth made me feel sick. He reminded me of a wolf now, although he was so much bigger and also had horns on his head.

'Oh, Bull!' said Grandmother. 'Get out of my garden immediately. You know you're not allowed to come in here.'

'RRRRRRRRRRH!' roared Bull.

He tore the mantilla to shreds and trampled it into the sand. Then he charged at the pansy-bed and dug it up with hoofs and horns.

'Shame on you!' cried Grandmother. 'Shall I summon Uncle Georg to punish you? Stop that at once! My poor pansies!'

In reply, Bull charged straight at the veranda. Screaming, I hid behind Grandmother's skirt. But he didn't come on to the veranda. Grandmother had closed the door. I heard the railings up the steps crackling as he set about them with his horns. His panting breath sounded so close, I could feel the heat of it. The floor shook.

'Shall I do even more damage?' roared Bull. 'Shall I knock down the whole house? Shall I bite your heads off, tear you to pieces and drink your blood? Shall I put you into the furnace in my belly and let you burn in the flames? Shall I . . .'

'Baal! Now I recognize you.' Grandmother's voice was trembling a little, but nevertheless sounded firm and dignified – as when she says prayers with us at night. 'Come to your senses for a moment and still the rage in your heart. Answer me . . . why have you come and what do you want of me?'

Bull stopped attacking the veranda railings. His voice sounded soft and ingratiating as he answered.

'Oh, Muscha! Although at the beginning of time you assisted my adversaries and have always striven to hurt me, although you have always agreed with my worst enemies, Abraham, Elijah and many others, and been their friend, I shall not break a flower in your garden or harm a hair on the heads of your descendants if you give me the little boy hiding behind your skirt thinking I can't see him. He belongs to me and I want him.'

I could feel Grandmother straightening up. She banged her stick on the floor and exclaimed: 'What makes you so bold, Baal!'

'I just want to have him,' said Bull. 'You can keep all your other grandchildren, though of course I ought to take his little brother. But I shall forget what the little one did because in his ignorance he was only aping his big brother.'

I clenched my fists round the folds of Grandmother's skirt as hard as I could and pressed my face into the black material so that everything round me was quite dark. A rare strength came from that skirt. I could feel it running down into my body and filling me with confidence.

'This child is under the protection of the Lord God,' said Grandmother. 'He's a good boy. He says his prayers every night. He doesn't fuss over his food any longer. He has learnt to clean his teeth and he never says bad words since I put him in the corner.'

'And you believe that!' said Bull, smiling scornfully.

'He's still so small,' said Grandmother, a trifle bothered. 'He'll probably improve as long as he eats properly and grows a bit.'

'And only this morning you yourself said that he's already a big man and it was shameful that he still wets himself. No, Muscha, stop talking against your better judgement and give me what is my right! My stomach is rumbling and my patience at an end.'

'Never!' cried Grandmother, again straightening up. 'Get thee hence, Baal, and fear the Lord God!'

'God's not the only one people owe faith and allegiance to. Even I have been feared and worshipped by the people of the earth. They have brought me sacrificial offerings and knelt before my image. But now this little boy has. . . .'

But Grandmother had no desire to listen. Trembling with fury, she interrupted Bull.

'In the name of the Lord God, Zebah, I command thee Baal, Beel, Belial! Get thee hence from my face, bloodthirsty idol, abomination of all the peoples of the earth! Go down into the underworld whence thou hast come! For thus saith the Lord that created the heavens: I am the Lord and there is none else.'

Grandmother seemed to grow, raising herself up towards the sky. When she banged on the floor with her stick, it sounded like a clap of thunder.

'But thou art nought but vanity. Cease despising the living God and defiling my house! The Lord saith: Although thou hast devoured many people, thou shalt not devour more.'

The louder and more threateningly Grandmother spoke, and the more her eyes flashed, the more Bull seemed to shrink and collapse, as if all his strength had run out of his veins. His body trembled, his teeth chattered and his face was distorted with rage. Great clear tears fell from his eyes. 'I want to have him,' he cried. 'You've no right to do this to me, Muscha. Listen now. . . .'

Grandmother held out her arm with the stick and mercilessly went on: 'See, I shall raise my hand against thee and visit thee. I shall bow thee down and put a bit in thy mouth and take thee out of the land of Israel. Thou shalt fall to the ground and I shall give thee as food to the birds whither they fly and to the beasts on the ground.'

At the same moment as Grandmother was proclaiming the latter invocation, two farm men came rushing into the garden. They had long switches in their hands and brought them swishing down on to Bull's back and hindquarters. He roared with pain, reared, and furiously tried to ward them off, tossing his head at his assailants. But they danced round him and avoided his attacks.

'Have you had enough?' Grandmother called out. 'Or shall I summon Moses and Elijah?'

Bull took to his heels. He charged through the garden hedge out on to the road and continued at a wild gallop in the direction of the byre, a hail of sand and stones swirling up behind him and the two farm men rushing shouting after him.

When he got to the ice-cellar, he once again turned his head. The last I saw of him was his weeping, distorted face looking at me with eyes full of pain and hatred. Then all three of them vanished in a swirling cloud of dust.

Since that event Bull has not put in an appearance. When we walk past the byre, we occasionally hear his sorrowful bellowing from behind the thick prison-like stone wall.

As soon as I close my eyes nowadays, his face, staring ominously at me, appears in the pattern of black patches of shadow gliding past. Sometimes he appears as a whole, just as when I saw him charging into our garden with his head lowered, smashing everything in his way, heavy, dark and as tremendous as a block of rock.

His image follows me everywhere. He has bewitched it on to me and I can't get it out of my thoughts or escape from it – as little as I can escape from myself. If I make a real effort to think about something else, it is rubbed out and disappears for a while, but as I go on thinking, the things I am thinking about are transformed and his face is there again. Although he's there in his dark prison, welded to the wall like a criminal, and can only tug on his iron chain, I feel that he is around me all the time, that he's lying in wait and threatening me. He's like one of those magicians Aunt has told us about, who can leave their bodies and wander around as they please, although their bodies are lying in a dungeon without moving.

I often see his horns sticking out from the bushes in the garden. When the light fades, the bulging jug on the wash-stand acquires his features, or a bull's head stares at me from the flowery cushion on the sofa in the dining-room. He's inside the heavy armchair standing immobile in the dim light. When Grandmother pours out tea, the spout of the teapot turns into his willie and the tea rushes out in a thick yellow stream, just like when he peed out there by the fence and we laughed at him.

One evening he stood for a long spell outside the window, looking into the nursery, his eyes glowing as if he were a ghost, and he was blowing bunches of dancing flames out of his mouth. He didn't disappear until I called Aunt and she closed the stove door and explained that it was only the firelight reflected in the window.

Once when Aunt was to leave the milk-can with Anna, we went up to the byre door and Aunt opened it slightly.

At first I could see nothing, because it was quite dark inside and it took a moment before I could make out the dirty stone walls, the empty stalls and the channel in the stone floor down which a little stream of brown pee was making its slow way towards the door. I thought the byre was quite empty, but suddenly there was a heavy panting sigh from the darkest corner, the clink of chains, and something over there rose like a black mountain.

For a moment the light fell on Bull's face. The eyes glared hazily and vacantly, as if he were vainly trying to remember where he was. He stayed quite still and seemed to be waiting for us to come closer. Then he thrust out his nose, sniffed and curled his upper lip into an ugly and ambiguous gesture – half kiss, half suppressed yawn – so that the moist pink gums were exposed. The memory returned only slowly, and the eyes started glimmering as if a green light had been lit inside them until they sparkled like lamps.

Then suddenly he tossed his head to one side, the iron chain rattled and his dark bellow echoed like an organ in the vaulted roof of a church. He stamped his hoofs on the floor and jerked at the chain round his neck like an angry dog. I snatched my hand out of Aunt's grasp and rushed outside.

IT'S LOVELY IN THE CHURCHYARD IN THE DAYTIME, and we often go there for a walk with Aunt and Mamma to look at the graves. We take the route along the edge of the forest on the Vendelä road, where there are lots of wild mushrooms, and we arrive at the dark forest grove that hides the churchyard when you look out over the fields from Grandmother's window. There's a stone wall right round it, edged with raspberry bushes and briar roses. To get in, you have to unlock the iron lattice-work gate with black dagger-shaped spikes all along the top of it. After the gate has swung screeching open on its hinges, and then closed again behind your back with a click, you are inside the churchyard. It's dark, cool and quiet. The spruces there are taller and closer together than anywhere else and make a dark vault that completely hides the sky. The sunlight trickles through the branches here and there in golden rays, but never reaches all the way down to the ground. Perpetual dusk reigns round the graves, the sandy paths between them covered with spruce needles and dead leaves, and here and there the needles are so thick on the ground you would think the ants had collected them up to build an ant-heap. But there aren't any ants there. When you turn away from the graves and look out over the meadow through the gap in the forest, it is beautiful. The trunks of the spruces are like columns of black stone and the branches hang down like black lace draperies. But out there everything glows with light, the fields shimmering golden brown, and far away the lake's silky blue surface opens out and the clouds roll woolly and dazzlingly white across the horizon. It's almost as if you were looking at the world through a window from somewhere else and as if that was why it seemed so beautiful.

Grandfather's father and mother, my great-grandfather and great-grandmother, must have been terribly big, because they have the biggest graves. They lie alongside each other in the middle of the churchyard, their graves like two huge beds with a little grass and some red and yellow flowers growing on them. The crosses are iron and decorated with metal wreaths. When you see them at a distance, you think they are real flowers and they seem beautiful, but when you get closer and feel them, you realize that they are stiff and as sharp as knives, and the whole wreath rattles horribly. Old Uncle Guido's grave is decorated with palm leaves, but they are also metal. On the front of Gromli's cross hangs a little metal box which looks like a nesting-box and has a glass window, inside it a candle and a picture of Jesus's mother, but the glass is broken, the candle never lit and her face is cracked and covered with horrid black wrinkles. Almost all the graves have similar black iron crosses. Uncle Lebrecht's grave looks almost like a doll's bed and the cross is no bigger than me, but then he was only a little boy when he died, although he was already an uncle.

I'm afraid of all these uncles and aunts lying there in their graves under the earth. When I'm standing in front of the graves, I feel they're looking at me from below, lying quite still on their backs, looking and listening to me walking around and talking up there. You can't see them, but if you were to scrape away the sand and earth covering the graves, you would catch sight of them. Then I would be so frightened, I'd run away. It's as if I were looking down into a deep black well and could just make out the reflection of two pale twinkling stars down there. Their eyes follow me all the time and I can't escape them. I think they're awfully upset about me. They're envious of my being allowed to run around and play up here in the light, while they have to lie still in the earth all the time and can follow me only with their eyes. If they could, they would quickly grab me and pull me down into the grave and never let me out.

The spruce forest is thicker behind the churchyard. Although that's what the place is called, oddly enough there's no church there. There's a cairn of stones and the ground is covered with mossy chunks of stone, the stones heaped all higgledy-piggledy just as if a giant had tipped out a load there. The moss is damp and slippery and comes off the stones in great chunks. Bracken and old man's beard grow there, and it's full of treacherous pitfalls and horrid black holes leading down to the underworld. No wall separates the cairn from the churchyard, because it is actually part of it. I've never dared climb up on it, because as soon as I even look in that direction, I'm frightened and have to turn my head away. At the top you can just see a gigantic stone between the spruce trees. It rests on the smaller blocks like the stone base of a barn and the top is quite flat like a sacrificial altar.

Up there live the Mare of Death and the Burying Swine, the spooks and ghosts and all the other monsters who occasionally come to visit Grandmother at night in our dining-room. You can't see them in the daytime, because then they've crept down under the graves and Death himself stays right down under the earth in the graves of the dead uncles and aunts. But when night falls, he comes up out of the earth and summons all the awful spirits up out of their holes. Aunts and uncles climb up out of their graves and the whole loathsome company of ghosts, spooks, vampires and skeletons gather up there on the flat stone to celebrate the midnight hour. It's horrible that the place is so near our home, and I often wake in the morning with the echo of their hoarse cries and howling wails ringing in my ears.

But now Death has left the graveyard. Grandmother has read to us about how he'll be coming when the Last Days are at hand. And now he's here. Anyhow, it can't be a real uncle.

The very first time, I saw him from only far away when I was out picking wild strawberries below thin Uncle Erni's house. He came out from behind the churchyard wall on the other side of the field and went on between the spruce trees along the little path that runs along the edge of the forest and then takes a short cut across the meadows over towards the Big House where Uncle Frans lives. He was enveloped in a long dark cloak and had a kind of helmet on his head. Now and again the cloak parted and a huge wing flapped behind his back, then disappeared again. He never rose in flight but went on moving along the ground with dignified swaying movements which seemed peculiar and horrible. Sometimes he straightened up to his full height, and sometimes he leant forward as if bowing. Despite this violent rocking, he didn't seem to get anywhere and he literally crept forward. When a tree or a bush hid him, a whole eternity went by before the rocking head and flapping wing appeared again between the trees.

What was most horrible of all was the eye in that pale face. You couldn't make out the features in the face because of the distance. The eye was as gigantic as a dragon's and jet black. It stared right across the field straight at me without looking away. Every time the face was hidden by a tree, I thought, now he's stopped looking, so he won't bother about me any longer and I needn't be afraid. But then the eye was there again, staring so craftily and nastily that in the end I could hardly raise my eyes or look out across the meadow. I felt he was coming closer, although he was still distant and had hardly got half-way across the field. There was still time to run away and find a safe place. But it was obvious he had no intention of turning round and going back to the churchyard. He was coming towards us and, to crown everything, in broad daylight.

One evening when I was playing on the veranda steps, I suddenly saw him and Uncle Georg coming through the gate and continuing along the sandy path straight ahead. As usual, Uncle Georg was trotting along with his back bowed and knees swinging outwards, a walking-stick in his hand. His pink face with its protruding moon-shiny beard and reflecting forehead was beaming. Now and again he peered benevolently up at his companion and growled with satisfaction. The latter was swaying along beside him like a ship's mast, wrapped in his black cloak right up to his chin. Sometimes it flapped to one side, spread out like a sail and revealed a clenched hand and an upside-down knobbly stick, the handle of which swept over the grass like a scythe. He swayed to one side, then straightened up, flung his gangling black leg forward in a huge bow and placed a creaking hooflike boot down on the gravel. Then the other leg followed with the sole dragging along the ground as if he were sliding on it. High above the billowing black folds of his cloak rocked the head crowned with fluttering white hair. I saw an iron grey, bristly moustache, a drooping swollen lower lip and a sharp crooked nose that shot out like an eagle's beak. The black dragon eye looked as if it were only glued to his face and didn't seem to suit it. As close as this it had a strange empty, dead look that frightened me even more. I reached for my teddy bear and wanted to run away, but Uncle Georg stopped me.

'Halt, little fellow!' he growled. 'Has no one taught you any manners?'

I stopped in terror, lowered my eyes and held out my hand.

'That's it,' rumbled Uncle Georg, patting my head. 'That was capital!'

The one standing beside him let out a peculiar chuckling, gobbling sound, like a turkey.

'Well,' said Uncle Georg, putting his hand under my chin, 'don't you know who this is? He's your great-uncle, like me. Shake hands with him, too.'

I could feel my cheeks burning and my face going red. Uncle Georg shouldn't think I didn't know who was standing beside him. The fact that he also turned out to be my great-uncle was bad enough and also somehow indecent and hurtful to us all. But Uncle Georg shoving me towards him was really mean, for I had no chance of escaping. I squeezed my eyes tight shut to overcome my desire to pull my hand back. Something bony and cold fumbled at my fingers and pinched, then I heard an impatient, annoyed sound which this time reminded me mostly of the bark of a dog. Before I'd had time to start back, he bent right down over me and kissed my forehead.

Confused, I freed myself and stepped to one side. I could still feel his bristly moustache and cold lips on my forehead, as if he'd glued them there, and in my nose was the musty smell of old clothes and mothballs.

'Can you tell me if your grandmother is up yet, boy, or is she still having her after-dinner rest? Do you think we could look in?'

'I don't know,' I mumbled in embarrassment.

'I don't know! What kind of answer is that?' growled Uncle Georg. 'Have you no tongue in your head, boy? Come on, Heinz, we'd better go in and see.'

The other one let out a hoarse hissing sound. Panting and clumping, they started up the steps, Uncle Georg first and he following behind, clutching on to the railing. His knobbly stick thumped and banged dully on the steps and the panes in the veranda windows rattled as if the whole house were shuddering with horror.

I fled round the house to the kitchen steps, my forehead still prickling and chilly where he had kissed me, and it made no difference when I tried to wipe it off with my hand. I picked a few leaves growing under the kitchen balcony, spat on them and rubbed my forehead for ages, but it was impossible to wash off the mark.

Although I was afraid, I was also curious about what was happening in there, so after a while I crept into the drawing-room. The table was laid and Mamma was giving them all coffee. Grandmother was in her armchair talking to Uncle Georg. The stranger was sitting right in among them all, sipping his coffee. He had taken off his cloak and was now wearing a crumpled black suit and a starched shirt with a huge bow under his collar which glistened greasily, frayed at the edges and drooping like a dead flower. When he lifted his cup to his mouth, his cuff slid out from his sleeve and shifted up his hand like a glove. He held the other hand tightly closed in front of his chest all the time, as if he were still annoyed and wanted to thump the table with it. The cup shook in his hand, the coffee spilling and dripping on to the table-cloth. He leant right over, slurping the coffee into him, and big drops stuck to his moustache and ran down the corners of his mouth.

The peculiar thing was that his face was quite ordinary if you looked at it from one side. There was a little winking uncle-eye with a red-rimmed eyelid under a fluffy white eyebrow. The corner of his mouth was crooked and wobbled as on a horse, and he had ugly bags of skin under his cheek and chin. But it was anyhow a human face just like old uncles usually have. Not until you went round him did you see the other face, where the dragon eye was, pale and immobile and which could only belong to a ghost. But when I'd looked at it for a while, I noticed that it seemed much more awful than it actually was. The eye I'd been so afraid of was only a black patch of cloth held on by a silk cord in the place where the real eye ought to have been. Now that I had seen through this swindle, from that direction, he really just looked like a badly made rag doll which was supposed to represent something horrible.

Grandmother leant forward and asked something and the guest replied with the same incomprehensible sounds he had addressed to me outside. When he did that, they all fell silent round the table and sat and watched. He went on for a terribly long time – you could see he was making a terrific effort to produce all those awful sounds and behave in as terrifying a way as possible. He swallowed, cleared his throat, sniffed, sometimes pulling out a large crumpled handkerchief, putting it to his nose and trumpeting like an angry elephant. He straightened up, pressed his lips together, his face turning as white as a sheet, and beads of sweat appeared on his forehead. The whole of his body shook with fury as he raised his clenched fist as if to strike us all – then something exploded inside him and the sound came rushing out so that spit scattered all over the place. But no human speech ever came out. He bleated, bellowed, yelped, grunted and crowed in the most peculiar and strange way, as if he had wanted us to think he was a wild animal who would gobble us up in one single gulp the very next moment. After he had frightened us sufficiently, he threw himself back on the sofa, shaking with laughter, but only a hoarse hissing came out of him, as if it had been a snake laughing. He never seemed to want to stop. The living half of his face contracted into friendly creases, he closed his uncle-eye tight and a large clear tear fell down his cheek and got caught on his moustache.

I could see the Grown-ups were appalled at their guest's rude and inappropriate behaviour. But they feared he would notice how afraid they were even more, so they pretended it was a perfectly ordinary coffee party and that the guest was behaving in every way he should. They didn't dare look at each other, and they laughed, though their laughter sounded rather forced. Only Grandmother nodded several times in a friendly manner at his incomprehensible torrent of words and when he finally stopped, she said: 'I hope you'll like it here with us, my dear.'

In the end the guest became so noisy and excited, his arm gesticulating so wildly, he tipped his cup over and knocked it to the floor. The coffee ran over the table-cloth and down his trousers and waistcoat. His face turned ashen and he picked up his table-napkin and waved it about without wiping himself clean – all the time letting out one angry cry after another. For the first time I heard him uttering real words now – perhaps he had given up acting or wanted to tease and annoy Grandmother even more. But he distorted the words and disguised his voice so that it was hard to understand what he meant. 'Die Die! Satan!' he shouted. 'Khe Khe Khe Die Die Muscha Khe Khe Khe!'

I really did think Grandmother would now lose patience at last and reproach him, yes, perhaps even ask him to leave. But she simply pretended not to hear or see anything and turned to Uncle Georg. Mamma took the table-napkin out of his hand and started wiping his clothes and the table. The broken cup was picked up and taken out to the kitchen, and he was soon sitting there with another steaming cup of coffee in front of him as if nothing had happened. Not until then did he stop quarrelling, just as if we had spilt the coffee and broken the cup, not him.

I tried to look into his mouth several times, to work out how he produced those awful incomprehensible sounds. His mouth is crooked, the corner on the side where the black cloth eye is contemptuously drawn down and quite still. His cheeks are hollow and become even more so when he opens his mouth. You can see two teeth, long and brown like a rat's, but behind them everything is murky and black. At first I thought perhaps he had no tongue, that it had been cut out or had rotted away and that was why he really couldn't speak. But I caught a brief glimpse of the tip of a tongue inside that black opening between his lips. It looked dried up in some way, standing on edge, lead-coloured like Aunt Louise's cockatoo's.

As soon as the guests had gone, I ran back to the nursery and told Tommy all about it. 'You've no idea how horrid he was,' I said. 'He had made himself look like an old uncle just to deceive us. But you could soon see that he wasn't a person, because only one half was alive and moving. The hand on the dead side was thin and knobbly like a skeleton's and the nails were blue. And then he had a huge black cloth eye on one side of his face to frighten us. Do you want to see . . . ?'

'No,' whispered Tommy, retreating cautiously. 'No, I don't want to see . . .'

'Of course you do,' I said, interrupting him and pulling the black plaid off Aunt's bed. 'I'll show you. This is what he did. . . .'

I tucked myself into the rug, sucked my cheeks in as hard as I could, frowned and swayed over to Aunt's armchair and sat down.

'I don't want to see,' whined Tommy. 'I don't want to. Stop it!'

But I wasn't listening. I was enjoying my hideous appearance to the full.

'This is what he did then, you see.' I waved my arm around wildly. 'Aarrgh! Ua Ua Ua Ua Ua Uaa!!! Then he flung his cup and saucer on to the floor so that coffee splashed all over the place and yelled: "Damn and blast da da Muscha! You will will die a Death die a Death die a Death Khe Khe Khe Ua Ua Ua DIE A DEATH!" '

I couldn't help it. I had to hit out at Aunt's sewing-box and it crashed to the ground, buttons scattering everywhere. I didn't want to touch the lamp at all, but that also overbalanced and started to sway. And although I leapt up and caught it just as it fell over, the lamp glass slipped out of my hands and smashed on the floor and paraffin ran all over my hands and spread into a large pool.

Tommy had rushed screaming out of the room. I closed the door, threw off the plaid and tried to wipe up the paraffin with it. But I didn't have time to remove the traces of what I'd done. Rapid footsteps were approaching, the door flew open and Aunt was standing in the room.

'How many times have I told you not to be nasty and torment Tommy!' she shouted, looking grimly round. 'Just look at this mess! Give me my rug!' She rushed over and snatched it out of my hands. 'To think that I can't leave you alone with Tommy for five minutes without you getting up to something! I've never known such an impossible child in all my life!'

I let her go on at me without arguing back. Naturally, what she said was true – I'd been disobedient. I never left other people's things alone. I'd broken the lamp glass and ruined her rug. I didn't care whether Grandmother would now have to spend the last of her money on buying a new lamp glass, or that Aunt's bedclothes would now smell of paraffin for ever and ever. There was no child on earth so impossible, stupid and troublesome as I am. I thought about nothing but spoiling things and tormenting people smaller and weaker than myself. A grown-up like Aunt would never have understood that if you had just been through something as peculiar and horrible as that coffee party just now, you also had to show your younger brother exactly the way everything had happened, otherwise he would never understand. Things always go like that for me. I just want life to be a little more exciting and fun, but then everything goes wrong, one misfortune follows another and everyone starts hating and loathing me.

'He was playing being Death,' said Tommy, who had come in behind Aunt, his eyes shining with delight as he listened to her scolding me. 'I told him he mustn't frighten me and he must stop. But he wouldn't and kept saying he was Death.'

'What?' said Aunt, now down on her knees picking up splinters of glass. 'Playing at being Death? I don't understand. . . .' She turned round, her eyes flashing.

'He said we all have to die,' Tommy went on, telling on me even more. 'And then he got angry and started yelling and throwing things. He shouldn't play like that. And I don't have to die although he says I do . . . because he's not really Death is he, Aunt?'

I had to explain everything. Aunt was so angry, she smacked my bottom and put me in the corner. After she'd cleaned up and got rid of the smell of paraffin, she called me over and started scolding me again. What kind of rubbish had I been putting into Tommy's head, telling him that nice uncle who had come to see them was Death? His name was Uncle Heinz and he was a real person, just like the rest of us. I was a naughty, bad-mannered child to make a fool of a poor cripple, who was not only that but was also my own great-uncle. What had happened to him was terribly sad and we had to be especially nice and kind to him. He had been living far away in the Caucasian mountains, where he had once been grooming a horse and had been careless enough to stand behind the horse's tail. When he had lifted the horse's hoof, he had been kicked in the face, so that he had had one eye kicked out immediately and he had been paralysed down one side. Ever since then, the uncle had been as he is now, and he can't help looking the way he does. There are some things you just don't joke about and Death is one of them.

EVER SINCE THAT VISIT, UNCLE HEINZ'S TALL BLACK figure has been swaying round here at Teerilä. Almost every day he limps past our kitchen window, no matter if the weather is fine or bad. You can be quite sure of seeing his shadow swaying past whenever it's pouring with rain, the gutters gurgling, the forest enveloped in steel-grey mist, and the Grown-ups just sitting around complaining about the weather. It's just the same when there's a storm, thunder or hail, and the sky and the earth are tussling with each other to such an extent that no one else dares go out. Then it's as though Uncle Heinz were particularly pleased. He blows himself up like a toad, his cloak billowing and swelling, his arms thrashing about, and he raises his stick and shakes it as if he were threatening the wind because it wasn't blowing hard enough or he was ordering the trees to wave their branches about even more wildly. Sometimes you would think it was a gigantic black bird flapping about out there, trying to get air under its wings in order to be able to take off and fly away.

When we're out for a walk with Aunt, we keep meeting him. He's always alone and he goes for terribly long walks. You often catch just a glimpse of him, like a little black sail between the fields, or far away from us, on the road where it stops and disappears into the forest. He's always enveloped in a black cloak, a stick in his hand which he holds upside-down as if wanting to trip someone up with the handle. Sometimes he's bareheaded, but usually he's wearing a soft hat that's pressed together at the sides and looks like a helmet. The turned-down brim hides his forehead and half covers the cloth-eye. His thin neck shoots out of the collar of his cloak and is bare and wrinkled like a vulture's. The funny thing is that you keep meeting him in places far away from each other and in quite different directions from home, while when he's in sight he never moves faster than at a snail's pace. Like a magician, he must be able to move from one end of Teerilä to the other in a second. When he's standing in front of Aunt emitting his incomprehensible shouts, his cloak swirling and slapping round him, I can't help thinking he's just deceiving us with all that limping. In actual fact he can spread out his cloak and sail away over the trees if he feels like it. But he does that only when no one's looking.

It's also odd that ever since he came here, you keep finding little dead animals on the roads, shrews, voles and moles. They lie there in the gravel on their sides or their backs, their eyes tight shut and their small mother-of-pearl teeth exposed in a helpless grin. You can't help picking them up and brushing the sand off their thick velvety coats. The colours shift so beautifully and they look so new and tidy that you don't want to believe they're dead. But they're cold and stiff and won't open their eyes or close their mouths, and their paws always curl up again, however much you pull and squeeze them. The strange thing is that there's never anything wrong with them – their coats are whole and you can find no trace of blood or injuries. I feel terribly sorry for the sweet little animals and would prefer to put them in my pocket and take them home to play with. But Aunt soon tells me to throw them away. You can get infected and die if you touch them, she says.

Then there are the crows that have suddenly appeared in flocks here at Teerilä. They follow Uncle Heinz on his walks. Sometimes they fly ahead of him, sometimes they come flapping behind him with heavy wing-beats and breathless cawing, to land in a tree-top just as he walks past. I once saw him standing in a field talking to them. The crows came soaring in from all directions and settled down beside him, on haycocks, on stones, on the barn roof and in the stubble down on the ground. They kept croaking and cawing and more and more crows kept coming, the ones that had been delayed behind the tree-tops in the forest and dived down on to the field. But in the end they must have annoyed Uncle Heinz, because he suddenly swore and shook his stick at them so angrily that the whole flock rose with a terrible racket. I've never seen such a gigantic cloud of crows in my whole life. They circled round above the field for a while, as if refusing to obey Uncle Heinz and go away, but when he raised his stick and threatened them again, the flock turned and soared away over the forest. You could follow their flight for a long time, until the birds could be seen only as small flickering dots against the light clouds and your eyes began to ache. Where had Uncle Heinz sent the birds and what had he ordered them to do?

There's an irreconcilable hostility between Uncle Heinz and all horses, but that's not surprising. He always gets down from the road or turns on to a forest path when he meets a horse-drawn cart. Once when he was in our yard and Ali drove in, Uncle Heinz screamed and flung his stick up as if wanting to crush both Ali's and the horse's head with it. The horse was frightened and backed away so that one wheel of the cart struck Baby's pram and tipped it over, but fortunately Baby wasn't inside it. Another time I heard Uncle Heinz shouting and bellowing at Kaima and Veikko, who had quite innocently stuck their heads over the fence, wondering why he was walking so oddly. The poor foals were so frightened, they galloped away to the far end of the meadow and wouldn't come up to the fence all day even when I called them.

I've gradually got used to Uncle Heinz. In some way or other he's begun to be part of Teerilä. You often see him sitting on Uncle Erni's veranda or beside Uncle Frans at the top of the sky-high staircase at the Big House. Once I was up there with Aunt. A whole gathering of aunts and uncles were having dinner at a long table, Uncle Heinz at one end of it. He had a large table-napkin tied round his neck and an oilcloth under his plate. The table-napkin was covered with splodges of spinach, yolk of egg and sauce. He bent right down over his plate and slurped his food in spoonful by spoonful. It fastened in his moustache and ran down the corners of his mouth and chin. When he puffed and coughed, drops of sauce, bits of carrot and cranberry preserve spurted about and stained the oilcloth around him. It was shameful to look at. He ate worse than a baby, but they all pretended not to notice.

Now and again Uncle Heinz comes to see us and sits in the drawing-room talking to Grandmother. Once I had lost one of my galoshes running across a newly ploughed field. When I got home, Uncle Heinz was there on a visit and the Grown-ups were having coffee on the veranda. Mamma and Aunt almost at once started scolding me about the lost galosh and sent Bernt and me to go and look for it. We found it quite quickly in a furrow where it had stuck in the clay. The next day I met Uncle Heinz by the ice-cellar. I tried to give him a wide berth and hurry quickly past, because I was alone. But he thrust his stick out and stopped me with a malevolent laugh. I stopped and waited, my heart thumping. It was awful being so close to him and alone. He had drawn himself up and made himself taller to frighten me even more. His hollow cheeks chewed away for a long time before any sound came and then suddenly he roared: 'Galosh di di!'

I jumped and looked up at him in confusion. It was obvious he would be annoyed if I didn't answer soon, but I couldn't understand what he meant.

He jabbed his stick into the ground and pointed at my feet. 'Galosh di di! Galoshesheshes Di di!'

I still couldn't grasp what he meant. I wasn't wearing galoshes that day because it was fine and dry.

'What?' I finally managed to whisper. 'What did you say?'

But Uncle Heinz was really angry now. He leant forward, seized my arm and shook me so that I thought my arm would come off as he kept on and on, more and more angrily shouting his incomprehensible 'Galosheses Di di!'

I clamped my mouth shut. Anger and fear made me as heavy and immovable as a sack of flour. Uncle Heinz couldn't lift me off the ground. I had his yelling face right in front of my eyes, saliva spurting out between his brown rat-teeth and hitting me on the forehead and cheeks. He was clearly going to gobble me up. I was just about to start screaming my head off when all of a sudden his power of speech came back. He said – jerkily and stumblingly, true, but quite clearly so that I understood: 'Galosh . . . where did you . . . find it?'

He had hardly got the words out when he let go my arm. I didn't bother to answer – he'd frightened and humiliated me so badly. I turned my back on him and fled.

Although Grandmother and Mamma are always friendly to Uncle Heinz and put something out for him whenever he appears, it's quite clear they don't like his visits. Mamma always draws a deep breath when Uncle Heinz has slammed the door behind him and is clumping down the steps. She leans forward and in a low voice starts saying something in French to Grandmother, and Grandmother smiles and nods in agreement.

That business of a horse kicking Uncle Heinz doesn't seem to me all. Behind that story must lie something very strange and perilous, as Mamma and Grandmother are so eager to keep it from us. Once when Uncle Heinz had been on a visit, I heard Grandmother say to Mamma: 'Of course it's sad to see. But sins bring their own punishment – you must remember that, Anni dear.'

Another time when Aunt Luscha was talking about holy things with Grandmother and I came into the drawing-room without them noticing, Aunt Luscha said: 'Then he said, I've done what I can, Heinz. I can't help you any more.'

Grandmother sighed and shook her head. 'Yes, yes, Luscha dear. All these orgies . . .'

'Dreadful, Muscha! Quite dreadful! She had no idea whatsoever. That he should be the death of her in that way. . . .'

Then Aunt Luscha leant across towards Grandmother and lowered her voice so that I couldn't hear anything. Grandmother nodded in confirmation and cleared her throat: 'You're right, Luscha. He was being the death of her, and she's hardly the only one whom he. . . .'

But she stopped speaking the moment she caught sight of me and called for Aunt. In a disapproving voice she asked Aunt to keep a sharper eye on me – my curiosity about everything forbidden and shameful was really beginning to go too far.

Supposing that feeling that Uncle Heinz gave me from the very beginning was right after all. . . . Death can have all sorts of disguises when he visits people and he doesn't have to appear as a skeleton, everyone knows that. If he's one-eyed and lame, that could be because of his fight with Grandmother a long time ago, by Mamma's sick-bed in Viborg, when Baby was born.

It's horrible to think that he's now appeared in Teerilä and sits in the drawing-room having tea with Grandmother. Why has he come and what does he want of us? It seems to me that both of them, Grandmother and Uncle Heinz, are on their guard and don't trust each other despite the fact they pretend to be so friendly. Sometimes when Uncle Heinz raises his voice and yelps in that peculiar way of his, it sounds as if he is bargaining for something. Grandmother raises her eyebrows and purses her lips with an offended, dismissive expression, but a puzzling little smile is nevertheless playing in one corner of her mouth.

SOMEONE IS WAILING FROM OVER BY THE LAKE. THE wail is shrill and long-drawn-out. You have to be very frightened or angry to be able to carry on and on like that. Perhaps it's someone calling for help. But nowadays we often hear desperate cries of distress of that kind. They always fade away after a while, and then nothing else happens, and you're cross with yourself for being frightened and expecting trouble. Perhaps it's some monster or ghost making fun of you in a human voice.

It's hot and dusty. Now and again there's a puff of wind that makes the rye crop rush over towards the lake. I seem to be tired and drowsy, the way you get when you've trudged along the road in the blazing heat for a long time. Aunt and Bernt are difficult, because they always want to walk so far and never get tired. The air is full of the scent of meadow flowers and newly mown hay and flies buzz angrily around me.

That cry hasn't gone away. Although I try to think of something else and pretend it's not there, I can't help listening. Then I see Aunt and Bernt are also uneasy, Aunt frowning and looking worried, as if something were wrong. Finally she stops and looks over towards the lake.

'What is it?' I ask her. 'Who's screaming like that?'

'Sounds like someone weeping,' says Bernt. 'Someone's hurt. Listen!'

Aunt doesn't reply. We stand and listen. It really does sound like someone sobbing and catching her breath, then it's quite silent and all I can hear is the buzz of flies all around me. But then the wailing comes back, rising and filling the whole world. It's not a human voice. Only a wild animal can wail and howl like that. I can see that the farm-workers over on the hayfield are horrified too. They're leaning on their pitchforks and looking over towards the lake. An old woman with a white kerchief drops her rake and comes running across the meadow in our direction.

As we hurry on, we meet Uncle Heinz. He sways up to Aunt, raises his arm so that his cloak spreads out like a wing and points in the direction he has come from. He keeps the other arm hidden under his cloak, protruding from his side as if he were holding something against his chest. 'Mother di di,' he clucks. 'Mother . . . scr . . . screaming.'

I see Aunt's eyes widening and she turns pale. She begins to question Uncle Heinz, but he shakes his head and waves his hand dismissively, as if he considers it pointless to go on with the conversation. With an impatient jerk, he turns his back on us, flings up his leg like a jumping-jack and lollops off towards Teerilä. He looks as if he's in a hurry and is afraid of not getting away in time. Ahead of us, that wail is still echoing, as if the forest itself were trying to stop him and was calling him back. But he has already disappeared round the corner in a cloud of dust and smoke.

Aunt suddenly increases her pace so that she's half-running. 'Quick!' she gasps. 'Perhaps we can help in some way. We must hurry. . . .'

I start running, but I'm soon left behind and give up because I'm hot and tired and have no desire to obey her. The distance between me and Aunt grows longer and longer, and soon she is far ahead of me, her white blouse already gleaming at the end of the sandy stretch of road in front of me. My feet sink in the sand and my sandals fill up with small stones and gravel. Bernt has also got left behind, but is half-way between me and Aunt. I'm cross and angry with them both. Why do they always run away from me like this, leaving me alone? They know

I'm small and can't walk as fast as they do. Two women hurry past me, calling out loudly, and when I turn round I see a whole lot of people running along the road. I'm soon the last of them all.

At last I'm there. It's the channel with the road bridge over it, the workers' cottages and the secretive little skerry out in the water with its light stones on the shore and its pines. It floats towards you without ever coming any closer. There are a lot of people crowded on the bridge, some of them hanging over the railing and looking down into the water. I look around for Aunt but can't see her at first. For a moment I catch a glimpse of her white blouse on the bridge, but then she's gone again. I find it hard to see because everyone crowds in front of me and they won't let me through. It's like in a dream when something horrible is happening but you can't understand what's going on. That wail rings in my ears, but I can't see who is wailing or even make out where the wailing is coming from. Everything here is wailing – yes, the bridge itself under my feet and the dark water rushing along down there. No one takes any notice of me. They're all occupied with what is happening. They hurry past me or stand in groups, turning their backs on me and talking eagerly to each other. I'm shoved to one side and they tread on my toes.

When ultimately I find Aunt, I'm stopped by a man in a torn shirt lying face down on the bridge with his head and shoulders under the railing. He is holding his hands out to someone down there. When I look over the railing, I can see a naked worker, the water up to his waist, his hair plastered down on his forehead. He blows his nose with his fingers and splashes his hand in the water to rinse off the snot. Then he raises his arms and grasps the other man's hands, climbs up over the railing and jumps down beside me. He's wet and smells of mud. Drops of water splash my face as, shivering, he brushes the water off his sunburnt chest and shoulders. It's amazing that he shamelessly stands there quite naked, only occasionally remembering to put his hand over that place, although lots of women and Aunt herself are looking on. But Aunt also seems to have forgotten he's naked, or else she's pretending not to notice, although grown-up women are usually so afraid of naked men. He is breathing heavily, pushing his straggly wet hair back off his forehead and pointing sometimes at the water under the bridge, sometimes at the shore, and sometimes at the cottages further away. The women listen to what he's saying with horrified cries and slap their hands together.

Then I'm standing with Aunt down on the slope to the shore. People are all standing round a woman lying on her back in the grass. She's the one wailing like that. She's been screaming all the time and just refuses to stop. Her face is dark and swollen, her eyes round and staring like a fish's. She seems to be fighting with someone, because she keeps rolling back and forth, kicking and striking out around her. Sometimes she pushes her stomach out and bends backwards as if throwing off something that's pressing her to the ground. Then she rolls round and the people nearest to her step aside in horror. I'm frightened she will roll down the slope like a log, but there's a stone in the way and she starts beating her head against it. It's horrible. She wheezes, her eyelids droop and the rough stone gets blood on it. In the end, some of the people standing round rush up and drag her off. Aunt supports her so that she has to sit up. She quietens and starts rocking to and fro, now and again feeling her head, looking at the blood on her fingers and whimpering quietly.

Someone proffers a cup and Aunt leans over her and tries to get her to drink. But the woman doesn't see the cup. She holds it against her teeth and smiles slightly in a strange way. Suddenly her eyes again turn staring and round, and with a shrill scream she leaps up and runs down towards the sea. It all happens so quickly I don't have time to take anything in until it's all over. They all rush down to the shore. The water ripples and gurgles. A dark bunch of people crowd round down on the shore. Then the crowd parts and two men come up the shore with the woman between them, her hair hanging over her face, covering it, her dress plastered like a rag round her body, a green leaf stuck to a breast that has slipped out. Although the men at her side are holding her arms and pushing her ahead, she is resisting them, arching backwards, tensing her arms, tugging and pulling to get free and run back down into the water again.

Suddenly Mamma and Pappa are standing in front of me. They're gasping and wiping the sweat off their faces. They've both got a big fluffy bath towel over their arms and Pappa has Mamma's bag in his hand.

'Where is he?' Pappa asks, leaning forward. 'Have they got him out?'

I can't make head or tail of anything. But other people push forward, surrounding Pappa, talking and fussing noisily. Then they all rush off towards the cottages, a little old woman in a black silk kerchief and striped apron running ahead of them, pointing with her hand and shouting. I see them disappearing into a dark little cottage.

THE COTTAGE ROOF HAS MOSS ON IT AND ONE OF
the windows has been mended with a piece of cardboard.
Fishing-nets hang drying along the wall, some red poppies gleaming below, and a black cat is sniffing at a pot of
dried-up fish. Two children with brown sunburnt faces
and flaxen hair are sitting on the steps, staring silently at
me with their light watery eyes. I creep slowly past them
up the splintered crooked steps and go inside to see what
Mamma and Pappa are doing in there.

It's dark and stifling, people either pressed round
the door or lined up along the walls. A pan is steaming
on the stove and an old woman stirring the fire, the
flames leaping and lighting up her wrinkled witch's
face. Over by the window where the daylight is pouring
in, two shadows are leaning over a big table. They look
as if they were kneading dough. When my eyes have
got used to the darkness I can see the faces and the
blackened walls around me. Now I can see that it's
Mamma and Pappa over there by the table, something
lying between them covered by a towel. Not until I
push my way forward do I see that it's a naked boy, no
bigger than me. Pappa is leaning over him and squeezing
his back with both hands, while Mamma is rubbing
his legs with the towel. It's awful to see how roughly
they're treating him. Mamma is rubbing so fiercely, she
looks as if she were trying to scrub the skin off him,
and every time Pappa squeezes, the boy lets out a dull
rattling sigh. I approach slowly and tug at Mamma's
skirt so she'll notice me. But Mamma just gives me an

impatient glance that tells me I must keep out of the way.

'Can you feel anything?' says Pappa, straightening up.

Mamma grasps the boy's ankle and lifts up his brown foot. His heel is a shiny pale yellow. The boy tries to kick with the foot to get free, but when Mamma lets go, the leg thumps feebly back on to the table and stays there in a peculiarly uncomfortable position with the heel outwards, as if the boy were too tired to move.

'His feet are icy cold,' pants Mamma. She presses her lips together and goes on rubbing.

I lean over to take a look at the boy's face but start back in horror, for his face is dark blue, like a ghost's, and flattened in some strange way. It's all so horrible, I creep out.

For a long time I wander about without knowing what to do. It's light outside. My eyes hurt in the sunlight and it's hard to look up. The wind rustles through the grass, the red poppies sway slowly, and a butterfly dances among the nettles round the stone base. The cat is licking its paws with its little pink tongue and the two children are still crouching on the steps. A little way away from the cottage where the grass slopes down towards the sea, the woman who had recently thrown herself into the water is sitting with some other peasant women. She has stopped screaming and is rocking back and forth, her hair down, and she has spread a towel over her head and is holding the corners so that she looks as if she's in a little tent. Her face is in the shadows and you can see only the eyes gleaming inside. You don't know what they're looking at.

After a while I find Bernt sitting down by the shore, picking at the gravel with his fingers, now and again taking up a stone and throwing it into the water. He tells me the boy had been playing up on the bridge. Perhaps he had climbed over on to the outside of the railing, perhaps simply leant too far forward under it to look at something in the water under the bridge – no one was there when he had fallen in. When his mother heard him screaming, it was already too late. He had drowned before anyone had had time to reach the bridge.

'Like this,' said Bernt, throwing another stone into the water. 'He sank and was gone, because he couldn't swim.'

We stare at the rings in the water gliding away from the place where the stone had plopped. A bubble glitters over there for a moment or two, then disappears, and no one can say any longer that the stone made a hole in the water.

'Then it was almost impossible to find him,' Bernt goes on. 'The water's so deep and it's pitch-dark down there. He was dead when they got him out.

'But it's not too bad,' he adds after a moment's silence. 'Pappa and Mamma will probably bring him back to life. They're working at it over there in the cottage. And soon, you'll see, he'll wake up, sit up and start talking. Just think how happy his Mamma will be then.'

'He's already moving,' I say eagerly, in confirmation. 'I saw it myself just now. Come on, let's go and see.'

But the boy still hasn't woken. Aunt has relieved Pappa at the head end. They seem to be in even more of a hurry than before. Aunt's face is glowing, beads of sweat coming out on her forehead as she keeps repeating the same strange movement, rocking back and forth as if at a mangle. The boy's body flops helplessly to and fro between Aunt and Mamma, the thin arms swinging up and down, extended and pressed back again against his chest. He's breathing all the time, now and then letting out a heavy sigh and tossing his head as if it hurt terribly somewhere. But his eyes are still shut. All the time I'm waiting – now, now he'll open his eyes, sit up and say: 'Stop messing me about! That's enough now!'

But nothing happens. It's the same all the time. As long as the Grown-ups keep on working at it, he breathes, moves and is alive. But as soon as they let him go, he's dead and lies there with his eyes closed and his arms and legs stretched out, as still and mute as the table top beneath him. In vain I stare at him, trying to catch the slightest movement of his fingers, the slightest little trembling of his eyelids, the lightest heave of his chest. Things start flickering before my eyes and I become cross-eyed.

The Grown-ups don't give up but go on working on him. They look tired and distressed, and relieve each other more and more frequently at the head end. The boy also looks as if he couldn't go on much longer. He is turning paler and paler until he's almost as white as the towel covering him. His arms go numb and move to and fro more and more slowly. More and more frequently the Grown-ups lift him up and turn him over. They make him hang with his head and arms over the edge of the table, squeeze him and thump his back so that he vomits up a mass of muddy yellowish-white water. No one bothers to wipe up the puddle and the Grown-ups tread in it.

It begins to be very quiet and empty inside the cottage, the men and women nodding at each other, leaving their places and pattering one at a time out through the door. All you can hear is the Grown-ups panting over by the table and the old woman clattering by the stove. I begin to grow sick and tired of it all. I curl up on a bench beside two women who are still sitting there whispering to each other. Whenever will the Grown-ups have finished so that we can go home? They can't be very good at it if they have to go on like that and can't bring the boy back to life! If you're sufficiently holy, you can wake the dead in a moment. You have only to go up to him, grasp his hand, lift two fingers to the sky and say: 'Talitha cumi.'

Yet it's much worse for the drowned boy than for Jairus's daughter. What does God do now when he sees that all Pappa's, Mamma's and Aunt's efforts are not enough? It would be a small matter for him to send a prophet, an angel, or Jesus himself here to wake the boy up. Sometimes there's a secretive rustling out there, the room expands and grows lighter, golden specks of dust dancing in front of the window. The next moment the steps will creak, the door will open and the whole room will be filled with dazzling light. But nothing happens. As usual, God doesn't care what's happening and does nothing to help the boy.

At last the Grown-ups are ready. Pappa fumbles with a match, trying to light a cigarette. Mamma folds up the bath towel and looks in her bag. Aunt is still over by the table, holding a little pocket mirror in her hand, blowing on it and rubbing it against her skirt. Then she holds it for a moment over the boy's mouth and looks into it. She does that several times, as if expecting to see something in the mirror. A round spot of sunlight trembles on the boy's forehead each time she holds the mirror close to his face, but as soon as she takes the mirror away, the spot of sunlight leaps over to the wall and hides away among the blackened beams in the ceiling. 'He's dead,' she says, handing the mirror to Mamma. 'God has willed it.'

Then they say nothing more, and they all silently pick up their belongings. I cautiously go over to the table and have a look. The boy is now lying on his back, quite naked, his body as white as ivory. Even his lips are pale and bloodless, as if a pane of glass had been pressed against them. His face is so lovely and stern, you're a little afraid when you look at it. You can see he's pleased they've at last left him in peace and that he doesn't want to be disturbed any more. And yet he is grieving. There's a glitter like tears beneath the thick eyelashes. Is he crying over what Aunt has just said, that he's dead, that God had willed it, and that all our attempts to wake him up have been in vain? His hands rest so heavily on the table – he'll never manage to lift them again. And yet his fingers curl inwards as if they wanted to close round something and hold on to it. Those half-closed fingers, still sunburnt and covered with scratches and scars, are just like my own. They look so helpless and are begging us to put something in them – a flower, a toy or, best of all, your own hand, then to stay sitting beside him without taking away the hand so that he doesn't have to be afraid.

Carefully, I raise my hand and poke him with my forefinger. I don't really know why I am doing it – I'm ashamed afterwards, because I hadn't anything to give him and was afraid to take hold of him. Perhaps I was just curious about what it would feel like to touch him, perhaps I wanted to see whether he really was sleeping so soundly that he wouldn't notice. That was when the strange thing happened. He stretched, turned his head towards me, thrust out his chin and wheezed deeply. His arm whisked across the table, fumbled for me and stayed hanging in the air. He was trying to say something. Some white sticky stuff welled up between his lips and ran down his chin.

I start back. 'Aunt! Mamma!' I squeal, for my hand feels strangely numb and cold. 'He's woken up. He's not dead at all. Don't you see?'

But the Grown-ups have seen nothing. They say the arm had slid down from the table because I poked him and they scold me for my inability to keep my hands to myself and that I can't even leave the dead in peace. Mamma wipes the boy's mouth, lifts up the dangling arm and adjusts his head in a comfortable position. Then they all stand looking at him for a moment as if saying goodbye.

'Come,' says Aunt, turning away. 'There's nothing we can do here.'

They take the towels and bags and walk towards the door. I reluctantly follow them after glancing one last time at the table where the boy is lying. I'm ashamed and soon turn my head away again, but all the same I have time to see that the boy is crying because we're leaving him. The Grown-ups can say what they like – it's cruel of us to leave him alone. Up to the very last moment he has trusted us to help him and only now when we are leaving him does he realize he is dead.

Outside, it's still stiflingly hot. A huge lead-coloured cloud is looming up on the horizon, the forest glowing against the dark cloud and the water in the channel as black as ink. But the sun's still shining, little tongues of flame winking and dancing on the water, the water-lily leaves glistening as if they were silver-plated.

Shuddering, I look down between the planks as we hurry across the bridge. Deep down below me, as if in a well between swirling foam and black logs, something pale brown and slimy waves at me, sometimes like flowing hair, sometimes like a waving hand. There's a rippling and gurgling all the time, a hum of voices penetrating up from below. What did the boy see down there? How deep is it down to the bottom? Would you touch bottom if you thrust your fishing-rod right down to the handle, or would you have to put lots of trees on top of each other? My head spins as I look through the cracks. There's a secret force in the bridge that sucks you downwards. If you weren't careful, you could take a false step and slip, a plank might break or give way beneath you, or without knowing what you were doing you might climb over the railing and throw yourself down into the depths. The same evil force also affects the Grown-ups, Pappa, Mamma and Aunt, as long as we're on the bridge. At any moment one of them might turn round, grab me by the scruff of the neck and throw me over the railing.

'Why are you dawdling so, Riki?' Aunt calls. 'We must hurry. There's a thunderstorm coming.'

There's a rumble far away. The cloud has grown and become even darker, covering half the sky like a blue-black wall. The light on the forest on the other side of the lake has gone out and the forest is silent now, brooding as if it were evening.

'You're always lagging behind,' scolds Aunt, taking my hand. 'We always have to wait for you.'

She walks faster without letting go of my hand. I run behind her, trip over and get up again. My arm hurts. Aunt is pulling it so hard, it might come off at any moment. Suddenly there's a flash as if a match had flared up and gone out again. Then the thunder comes. It never seems to stop. It bounces up and down and crashes down into the forest and splits apart far over on the horizon with a furious bang.

We rush home. The sunlight vanishes, the colours around us fade and it grows dark as if it were already evening. The wind pulls and tugs at Aunt's skirt, swirling the dust up on the road and blowing it into my face. The trees rustle and sway back and forth. They bend over, lifting their branches so that the leaves are turned inside-out and glisten like silver paper. Sometimes it's dead quiet, the wind dropping and all the trees standing straight, without moving, waiting. Then they start rustling and soughing again, twigs and leaves swirling round, the trees whipping furiously to and fro. Over by the channel and the cottages we've left far behind us, now enveloped in grey mist, thunder and lightning are ceaselessly rumbling and flashing. I can see the lightning flaring up into the dark cloud and striking down like blue whisks of fire.

When we've got to the avenue, it starts raining. At first there's only a rustling in the leaves, as if they were full of nibbling mice, the light dusty ground under our feet filling with dark spots, and a few heavy drops of rain strike my forehead. But the next moment there's a persistent roar all around us, increasing more and more in strength. Everything turns a shimmering silvery white and the rain descends on us like a waterfall. Pappa wants us to get under a tree to wait until the worst is over, but Mamma and Aunt cry out that we mustn't. The lightning may strike the tree and kill us all.

As we stand there while the Grown-ups argue about what we ought to do, Uncle Heinz appears in front of us. He is soaking wet and crumpled, his cloak hanging slackly around his shoulders. He's become even taller and thinner, his moustache drooping and his hair plastered over his forehead. Water is pouring off him as if he had just stepped out of a well. Despite his dreadful appearance, he looks extremely pleased, again and again lifting up his face and letting the water wash over it, opening his mouth and swallowing the water. 'Ha ha!' he cries, contracting the living half of his face into horizontal creases. 'Ha ha!'

I don't understand what the Grown-ups are saying to him, but their tone of voice and their expressions show that they are reproaching him for his wild joy. Aunt even raises her hand and points to the sky. But then Uncle Heinz turns angry. He bellows and flings up his stick. The ground around us flares and the crash that soon follows is so loud, I have to squeeze my eyes tight shut and crouch down. When I open my eyes again, I see the top of a birch in the avenue we've just run past is coming down. The huge crown of the tree slowly turns upside-down and disappears with a dull crash behind the billowing mass of foliage. Then the rustle of the rain increases and it pours down with redoubled force.

'Hurry up now! Run!' cries Mamma, rushing away along the avenue. We follow her until our ankles are splashing in the stream rushing ahead where there had been a road before. Uncle Heinz disappears behind the silver curtain of rain in the crash and bang of thunder.

WHEN SUMMER IS OVER AND THE SMALL BIRDS gather in great flocks on the stable roof to fly south, the aunts and uncles all disappear from Teerilä. The houses are silent and empty, staring sorrowfully at you with their black window-panes. When you creep up on to the veranda and put your face close to the reflecting pane, you can just catch a glimpse of what it looks like inside. In big Aunt Lala's house the curtains are drawn and you have no means of knowing what's happening inside, but at Aunt Luscha's house the dim living-room appears through the veranda window and you can see the dark oak table, the still armchairs leaning back, the wall-clock with its pendulum no longer swinging to and fro. A half-smoked cigarette has been left in the green ashtray on the sewing-table in front of the window, the ring of Aunt Laura's lipstick still there on the squashed paper mouthpiece. I'm scared as I stand there looking. There can't be anything but ghosts living in the house, sitting in the armchairs, creeping over the dark red carpets and gathering round the big table in the evenings. Supposing one of them suddenly appeared before I had time to run away!

It has also grown quiet round thin Uncle Erni's house and Uncle Alfred's house down by the lake, only the spruces rustling sternly and the autumn leaves swirling along the sandy paths, where no more aunts and uncles will stroll. Finally the Big House and the Falkenheimer aunts' house are also vacated and they all leave. Huge loads with mountains of cupboards,

beds, sofas, wash-stands and pails lurch screeching past
our windows. The black carriage with red spokes comes
rolling by, Uncle Frans's black slouch hat and snow-
white beard just visible inside, and Shura and Vova
lean out to wave to us. Then fat Uncle Erni comes
in a purring red car, the three Falkenheimer aunts
in the back, Aunt Olga, Aunt Helene and Aunt Lina,
all looking like cobras through their lorgnettes. But
they're so heavy the car can't get up the little hill
by the ice-cellar in front of our house. Just as it gets
to the top, it starts sputtering and hissing and stops
with a bang. Then it rolls faster and faster backwards
down the hill again. You can see the aunts raising
their lorgnettes and putting their huge bird's-nest hats
to rights. Three times, fat Uncle Erni tries to get up
the hill, but each time the car rolls back again. Then
he lifts the bonnet, leans over so the top half of his
body is in the car's insides, and wrenches and swears.
The Falkenheimer aunts remain seated in the back,
silent and still like divine idols, staring through the
horn rims of their lorgnettes. Finally, a tall grey-clad
uncle comes running up. Fat Uncle Erni stands up and
you can see them opening and closing their mouths as
they shout at each other. Fat Uncle Erni sticks out his
stomach, throws out his hands and draws signs in front
of the other uncle's eyes with the wrench. The grey
uncle points commandingly hither and thither. Then
fat Uncle Erni shrugs and gets up beside the grey-clad
uncle at the wheel. The car door slams and to my
astonishment I see the car chugging smugly away up
the hill and disappearing round the corner with three
huge black hats bouncing in the back. Not until then
do I realize who the grey-clad uncle is. It is Uncle
Fabian.

Then everywhere is empty and silent. You can see
nothing but the farm girls going to and fro between the
stable and the byre and the farm men ploughing out on the
fields. The weathervane screeches round and the birds

circle below the grey clouds as if in a hurry to get away. Bernt and I spend all day searching for wild mushrooms in the forests. It's cold and wet, the branches of the birches full of drops of water like glass pearls. The moss gurgles at every step and the ground is strewn with yellow and orange leaves, making it look like a panther's coat. When we're back home, we help Aunt to clean the mushrooms and cut them into lovely white cubes. Then Aunt threads them on to a string with a big needle and hangs them above the stove to dry.

But it has become more and more difficult to find wild mushrooms in the forest, and nowadays our baskets are almost empty when we come home. The moss and leaves on the ground are often covered with rime frost and in the dark puddles you find thin triangular slivers of ice resembling pieces of a broken window-pane. The grass stems and sallow twigs leaning over into the puddles are fused into threads of ice that remind you of spun glass. Some of the puddles are covered with a dull milky crust of ice and, when you step on it, you crack it under your foot. There's no water under the ice, just empty air. Sometimes you stand in front of a bush, its leaves shimmering in crimson red, golden brown and lemon yellow, the branches and edges of leaves powdered with rime frost, and everything is so beautiful that you just can't stop looking. But the mushrooms are in horrid rotting heaps on the ground. The ones still standing have also darkened and shrunk round the edges, and when you pick them they fall apart and turn into a slimy mess between your fingers.

There's less and less food in the world and soon there'll be no food left at all. Mamma keeps going to Viborg and doesn't come back until after dark. Sometimes she goes the whole way on foot. Mamma and Grandmother are cross with Uncle Georg because he never wants to give Mamma a lift in his carriage into Viborg. But before thin Uncle Erni went away, Mamma quarrelled terribly with him about milk and flour and other food, and thin Uncle Erni didn't want to give us any at all. Since then, Mamma and Grandmother call him 'The Rich Man'. Nowadays we always have that horrible blackish-brown porridge that looks like the porridge in the bowl thin Uncle Erni's dog usually eats out of. It's horrid and coarse and tastes of paraffin. I feel sick and want to throw up whenever it's in my mouth and I can taste the paraffin. But Aunt makes me swallow it spoonful by spoonful. What will God say when he sees what a fuss I'm making, trying to spit out my porridge? Don't I remember the story about the girl who stamped on the bread? There are hundreds of thousands of children who don't even get porridge like that and who would weep with joy if they were given a spoonful.

Sometimes Uncle Georg appears in his oilskin, his great knobbly stick in his hand. He stands in the hall doorway and asks for Grandmother. But he doesn't argue with Grandmother about the War any longer, because things have gone very badly for Nikolaschka. He's no longer the Tsar of all Russia but has been driven out and turned into a dog. Bernt showed me a picture in the newspaper where you could see how Nikolaschka had fled. He was wearing a general's hat, his face was still all right and the eyes were looking sorrowfully at me above the black beard, but his whole body was already hairy and thin and ugly like a mongrel's. He had his tail between his legs and was scuttling away on all four paws to get away as quickly as possible. Grandmother and Mamma said that Nikolaschka had now received his punishment, but Aunt was sorry for him and wept as she kept saying: 'To think they could do such a thing to their own emperor!'

Uncle Georg says nothing at all. Perhaps he's frightened. He never mentions Nikolaschka's name any more, and when Grandmother occasionally talks to him about the War, he just shrugs his shoulders and mumbles: 'Weiss der Kuckuck!'

IN THE SUMMER MAMMA BOUGHT A PIG. HIS NAME was Jonah and he was roughly the size of a dog. He had flapping pink ears, a smooth cylindrical body covered with fluffy white bristles and neat little cloven trotters like ballet shoes. I soon got very fond of Jonah. He used to gallop up and down the road in front of our house, grunting so funnily, and flapping his great pink ears, that you were at once cheered and started laughing and felt like trying to catch up with him. But although Jonah's legs were small and short, he scuttled away like a hare and I never caught him. Sometimes when you stood still, he would come up to you with good-humoured grunts, nudging your knee with his wrinkled snout and looking trustfully up at you with his little black slanting eyes. Then he would turn, press against your leg and rub himself against it. His little round hindquarters wobbled and shrugged up and down so amusingly.

I once tried to ride on Jonah, but I had hardly got astride his back, which felt as firm and smooth as a hard stuffed sofa cushion, before he flew off with me like a torpedo. It was impossible to stay on his back, for there was nothing to hold on to. The next moment I was lying on the dirty road, covered with mud, watching Jonah strutting back with that coquettish curly tail disappearing in the distance.

Although Jonah likes playing nasty tricks so that you get as dirty as he is and get scolded for it, he likes you. Sometimes he runs after you, squealing and whimpering, and he is terribly pleased if you pretend to be afraid and run away. One day he followed us through the kitchen right into the living-room, and it was great fun hearing his little trotters pattering about on the floor, and seeing him sniffing at the chair legs and thrusting his snout under the piano to find out what might be hidden underneath it. But Grandmother was terribly cross when she came into the living-room and saw who had come to visit us. She grabbed the bell from the table and rang it so that Aunt, old Njanja and Kirsti came rushing in. Jonah was scared and rushed in under sofas and chairs. He dirtied the curtains and tipped over the three-legged mahogany table so that the things on it all fell on the floor. Then he got entangled in the lace table-cloth like a dancer and rushed out on to the veranda and disappeared down the steps with the cloth flapping like a white wing.

Grandmother asked what we thought we were doing, letting a pig into the house. Didn't we understand what kind of creature a pig was? The dirtiest of all animals, the epitome of dirt and filth! And afterwards Aunt scolded us terribly and tweaked our hair in turns. When Mamma came back, we had to wash our hands and promise never to touch Jonah, otherwise we should get the most horrible diseases in the world.

Ever since then, Jonah hasn't been allowed to play with us, but he takes no notice of that. As soon as he sees me, he lets out a whimpering cry and comes running after me, his pink ears flapping and his whole body shaking and trembling with delight at our reunion. It is very difficult just to go on walking without looking round and stopping. That's as if you no longer knew Jonah. I'm terribly sorry for him and don't want to offend him. 'Jonah,' I say. 'I like you all right. But Grandmother and Mamma have told me not to play with you. You mustn't be cross with me because of that.'

But Jonah takes no notice of what I say. He trips up to me and nudges my knee and then I have to scratch him behind his ear and pat his chubby body. Then I run away from him as fast as I can, feeling heavy inside and I'm afraid someone has seen us through the window.

Grandmother also said Jonah must not come into the garden and she is cross if she sees that Kirsti has let Jonah out of the little house Aunula has made for him. Jonah actually does a lot of damage. He digs up the flower-beds worse than a mole, bites off the flower heads and pulls long pieces of roots out of the soil. Sometimes he makes such a mess of himself that you're appalled when you see him, his face right up over his ears as black as a Negro and his body painted with great slate-grey patches of mud, cakes of earth and mud sticking to his bristles. Once when Jonah tried to get into the garden when Grandmother was taking a walk there, she gave him such a rap on the backside with her stick that he started squealing and screeching like a small child. Kirsti rushed up and got hold of him. She took him in her arms and carried him away as he sobbed and whimpered with his snout against her cheek.

For Kirsti loves Jonah. And Jonah likes Kirsti best of all. When she comes out on to the kitchen steps with the bucket, Jonah starts grunting and squealing in his partition of a stye. He gets up on his hind legs, puts his front trotters on the top plank and looks out. When he's let out, he rushes up to Kirsti, squealing shrilly, and follows her to the trough where she empties the bucket. He dances round her, tossing his head hither and thither, and is so funny you can't help laughing helplessly. Kirsti looks after Jonah the way a baby is looked after. She scrubs him, dries him, brushes his pink chubby body so that the fluffy hairs shine like silver and lie smooth and beautiful along his back. When Jonah is really polished and shiny, she takes him in her arms and sits down on the kitchen steps. Jonah wriggles his short fat hind legs about to make himself more comfortable on Kirsti's arm and puts his head on her shoulder. He blinks sleepily and contentedly and smacks his lips now and again, just like a baby when it's full. Kirsti rocks slowly back and forth and strokes his back, putting her lips to his transparent pink ear and mumbling: 'My darling little pet! Poor little, poor little Jonah!'

Now and again Jonah's ear twitches. It folds over quite lightly, then sticks up and spreads out so that he can listen better to all the pet names Kirsti whispers into it.

One evening when I went into the kitchen, Kirsti was sitting on a stool with Jonah in her arms, and she was crying. She turned quite pale and screwed up her mouth when she saw me. Then she quickly put him down on the floor and seized my arm. She said I mustn't tell anyone she'd had Jonah in the kitchen. It's so cold out there at night and Jonah freezes. If I dared tell on her, I would see something more horrible than anything I'd ever seen before. She took the big carving knife out of the cupboard and held it up in front of me. Then she lifted Jonah up and let me hold him in my arms for a while. It was like holding a large heavy cushion, for Jonah had grown a lot. He kept kicking me with his trotters and finally twisted out of my arms. He also smelt rather unpleasant, so I let him go and allowed him to slide down to the floor. Kirsti dug three lumps of sugar out of her apron pocket and put two into Jonah's mouth. He quickly gobbled them up with a crunching noise and a small belch. She gave the third sugar lump to me and then said with an awful glint in her eye that I must remember what she'd said.

I didn't tell on Kirsti, but somehow Grandmother and Mamma have found out that Kirsti takes Jonah into the kitchen at night. I heard Mamma complaining to Grandmother. She said it was really going too far to have a pig in the kitchen where all our food is cooked. Anyone as dirty as Kirsti ought to be dismissed. Jonah was moved out of his little house behind the kitchen steps and now he lives in a small partitioned bit of thin Uncle Erni's piggery behind the drying barn. Several times a day you can see Kirsti limping down the little hill by the ice-cellar with the bucket in her hand. She's taking food for Jonah and stays away so long Grandmother has to go without hot water for her tea and Njanja has to stoke the fire in the stove herself to heat up Baby's gruel. Kirsti doesn't even speak to me any longer. Her lips are pressed close together and she has red patches on her face as she glares horribly whenever I rush through the kitchen. I'm sure she thinks I betrayed her to Grandmother and Mamma. When I meet her outside the house, I always give her a wide berth.

I don't really understand why Grandmother dislikes Jonah so much and has banished him completely from the house. True, Jonah is a pig, and like all pigs has some rather dirty and off-putting habits. But he's also a prophet, one of God's chosen, and therefore sacred, so he should be treated with respect even if he does occasionally disobey God. Grandmother has told me how he once refused when God ordered him to go to the great sinful city of Nineveh and prophesy its downfall. His punishment was to be thrown into the sea, where he was swallowed by a whale. For three days and three nights he lived in the whale's belly before being spewed up on land and becoming good and obedient again. I'm sure it's rather creepy that he has now manifested himself here with us, because you can't really know what errand God has sent him on this time and whose downfall he is to prophesy. Is it because of Jonah's disobedience that Grandmother treats him so badly, or hasn't she even recognized him? Once when she heard me talking about Jonah with Tommy, she was cross and said: 'Stop that talk at once! You're breaking the first commandment and blaspheming against God. There are things that are sacred and he does not tolerate joking about them.'

Later on I heard Grandmother asking Aunt: 'Whoever thought of calling that horrible pig Jonah? Is that supposed to be a joke?'

Aunt replied that she didn't know, and that the pig had always been called Jonah, although for her part she found it offensive that a pig should be called after a prophet. Grandmother sighed and said it was a sign of the times.

NOW WINTER HAS COME AND THE WORLD IS covered with a layer of snow as soft and white as cotton wool. It's absolutely quiet outside the window. The trees look like white coral and all the colours have gone, so you can see nothing but silver grey and white whenever you look out.

In the morning Aunt comes into the nursery and tells us the pig is to be slaughtered that day. Kirsti is ill. She hasn't slept a wink all night and has done nothing but cry about Jonah having to die, because it's in her nature to like animals more than people. She's lying on her bed with her face to the wall and the kitchen is cold, the stove out and the dishes not yet washed. Njanja and Aunt have had to carry in wood for the stove to make porridge for us.

Then I have to play with Tommy in the snowdrifts outside by the kitchen veranda. We're cold, our faces frozen over and the frost nipping our cheeks and noses. We don't feel like moving, but just stand with our shoulders hunched up, hiding our heads inside our turned-up collars. The snow crunches under our feet. The road is hard and slippery, the sleigh-tracks glistening like icing sugar with cotton-wool snowdrifts rising on each side. Your mitten sinks deep down and, when you pull it out again, it's as if you had sugar icing all over it.

I'm sorry for Jonah. He's always such fun and so happy, and I like him so much, although recently I haven't been allowed to show it. I'm a little frightened about what's going to happen now, because Grandmother doesn't seem to be on God's side at all in this matter, but is more like the nasty Queen Jezebel who let the Lord's prophets be seized and slaughtered when they foretold the downfall of Israel and the house of Ahab.

On the other hand, it's nice to think about having something really good to eat again. My mouth waters when I see those pink and white slices of pork lean over and fall from Grandmother's knife, and I feel the delicious tender crisp crackling of roast pork crunching between my teeth. Jonah has really always looked so sweet and appetizing that you've felt like eating him up, especially when he had just been washed and brushed and was sitting on Kirsti's lap. The thought of all that pink rosy tubbiness makes me even hungrier than I already am. I remember the marzipan pigs the Russian aunts used to bring with them from St Petersburg. Oh how I loved that kind of pig! It had a blue bow round its neck and looked so joyfully and kindly at you that you had to kiss its snout and then you couldn't help biting off the ears, the tail, the feet and finally the whole head – and suddenly there was nothing left of the pig and you were rather disappointed. Then you were angry with yourself because the whole pig was already inside your stomach, for you would so like to have held it in your hand again and eaten it up all over again.

Suddenly we hear Jonah's desperate scream from over by the barn. He's screaming like a little child when it has been terribly frightened and no longer knows what to do. It's horrible to hear, because the squeals get shriller and shriller and more and more piercing and in quicker and quicker succession. Sometimes it sounds as horrible as a circular saw or the screech of the tip of a knife against a plate. Your teeth go numb and you have to screw up your eyes. Someone is being horribly nasty and is hurting Jonah, and Jonah has never thought anyone could do such a thing to him. He's screaming for help. He's calling for Kirsti, for Grandmother and Aunt, for me and Tommy, for everyone who lives here at home and whom he knows, because we shall come

rushing to rescue him from the murderers' claws. For
Jonah doesn't want to die. He wants us to take him
in our arms and console him, caress him and blow on
his sores so that they stop bleeding and hurting. That
scream is quite red. It comes flying from over there by
the barn and howls round our house in flaring coils. It
crashes into doors and rattles against the window-panes.
But everything here at home remains silent; the fire in
the stove glimmers in the kitchen window and you can
see Njanja doing things inside and bending down to lift
something up. The other window-panes stare vacantly
and dark out on to the snowy yard. For Jonah's death
has been decided on – nothing can prevent it. No one
dares raise a finger to help him because Grandmother
has condemned him to death. But Jonah doesn't know
that, otherwise he wouldn't scream like that.

'Now Jonah is dead,' I say when at last it is quiet.

Tommy doesn't answer, and when I go closer, his
face framed by his big winter cap with side-flaps and
ear-flaps of catskin is quite wet and glistening.

'You mustn't blub because Jonah's dead,' I say. 'We
haven't any food left. It's war, you see. And now we have
to eat Jonah up, because we haven't any other food.'

Then Tommy's really blubbing. 'I don't want Jonah
to be dead. Jonah is nice. Why didn't you go and help him
when he screamed?'

'You're silly,' I say. 'What could I have done? Do
you think the butcher would have obeyed me? It's
Grandmother who decided he was to die.'

But all the same I feel very uneasy. It's nevertheless
as if Tommy were right. I ought to have run to the barn
when Jonah cried out for help, and it wasn't because I
realized it would have been no use that I didn't, but
because I didn't want to.

In the afternoon Mamma sends Bernt and me with a
message for Uncle Georg. On the way home we make a
detour past the barn to see what happened to Jonah. But it's
all empty and quiet there and there's nothing to be seen.

The snow is trampled and covered with small red spots as if it had rained blood. In the middle there's a big hollow, its edges shining a pink flamingo red and the bottom like dark red candle grease. It's beautiful and horrible at the same time, because the red shines so brightly in the clean white snow. It's as if a fairy-tale bird had perched in the hollow and coloured the snow.

As we are going home, we see it has also rained blood along the road, not much, only a few little spots, as if someone had squashed a cranberry with his heel. The spots lead right up to our kitchen steps, and on the balcony Njanja is standing in front of a large saucepan stirring it with a whisk. Inside it is Jonah's blood, foaming and bubbling like whipped gruel, and horrid rubbery black threads are dangling from the whisk.

We have little blood-pancakes for dinner. They are ugly and black, as if they'd been burnt and turned into charcoal, but when you eat them they are tender, juicy and warm, melting against the roof of your mouth. At first they taste a little peculiar, but when you've had a few, you just want some more. Aunt keeps coming in with the dish heaped with more steaming little pancakes, neatly piled up on top of each other like the coins in Grandmother's money-box. We all eat and the dish soon empties, and Aunt fetches some more. We're all awfully hungry, because that morning we'd had only leavened bread with no butter and that disgusting brown porridge tasting of paraffin. When at last we're full and our stomachs feel really tight and a wonderful warm numbness fills our bodies right down to our toes, Grandmother clasps her hands and thanks God for the food he has given us today. Mamma talks about how grateful we must be for having this pig and that there are other children who are starving to death and have to make do with rats and crows, because their parents can't get any better food for them. Then Bernt says he has read in the newspaper that the Germans eat little children in Belgium. But Grandmother knocks on the table and orders Bernt to be quiet, for that's all a devilish lie the English have made up.

Then Njanja comes in with a big dish. It's covered with a white table-napkin. And when Grandmother lifts off the table-napkin, there is little Jonah's severed head, just like John the Baptist's head on a dish. Grandmother looks at the head and the rosy trotters and talks for a long time with Njanja about how they are to be preserved. Then finally she orders it all to be taken down into the ice-cellar.

But then there's a terrible noise in the hall, the door is jerked open with a crash and Uncle Georg stumps in in his hairy black sheepskin coat with rime frost on his beard and eyebrows. Steam is rising from him as from a horse and his face is scarlet. He puffs and pants, flings off his fur cap and wipes his bald head with his handkerchief.

Grandmother asks him if he would like some blood-pancakes, for there are a few left, but Uncle Georg raises his leather glove dismissively and hurriedly explains something to Grandmother and Mamma. You can see that he is angry, because his beard is shaking. He flings his arm out roughly as if sweeping away a number of invisible opponents, and almost every other word is 'Verdammte Kerle!' or 'Zum Kuckuck!'

I don't understand what he's saying, because he's rumbling so terribly and Grandmother soon looks at us and tells us to go into the nursery. Before we've got out of the door, I see the Grown-ups' faces turning white with terror as they listen to Uncle Georg. Grandmother starts up in her armchair, raises her eyebrows and the creases in the corners of her mouth tremble. Mamma throws out her hands and her eyes fill with tears. Aunt presses her lace handkerchief to her mouth as if to stop a whimpering sound coming out.

I can't sleep and lie awake in bed for a long time. The darkness outside is thick and black as in a cave, as if there were no sky above our house at all. The night is full of uneasy stray noises calling and answering each other – sometimes slow and far away, so you're not sure whether you've heard anything or whether you imagined it all, and sometimes so close and clear that you start up with terror. Sometimes it's like the echo of innumerable steps. The snow crunches out on the road, sleigh-bells jingle, a horse whinnies and you can hear swearing and arguing voices hastily retreating into the darkness. Then suddenly there's a shot over in the forest, a dog barks far away and everything sinks again into silence, as if the darkness itself were holding its breath, waiting for something. Only the wind whistles monotonously, whining round the house.

As I listen to the sound, I notice it isn't the wind complaining and whistling like that. It's someone crying and wailing. Sometimes there's a sob and the sound of someone catching their breath, then a subdued whimpering and crying starts up again. The crying is not coming from outside but sounds quite close. Sometimes someone's crying right under my bed, sometimes lamenting and moaning in the wall or up behind the damper on the tiled stove, as if the whole house were lamenting and complaining, mourning the death of Jonah.

I see Kirsti in front of me, awake in the little servant's room behind the kitchen. A flickering candle stump lights up her flat lined face with its high cheek-bones and sinewy neck, so the hollows above her collar-bones look like triangular holes. She is holding Jonah's severed head in her dark hands which are as rough and heavy as spades.

The candle flame recedes, shrinks together into a little blue spark and the shadows rise menacingly in the corners. Kirsti lifts Jonah's severed head up in her cupped hands as if on a tray and breaks out into a piercing lament. The monsters over in the forest answer her. They screech, neigh and bellow so that I hide my head under the covers in terror. They rise up out of the earth in hordes and come lolloping out of the forest. They crowd round Kirsti's window to look at little Jonah's head and trotters that Kirsti is showing them. They look at each other with dismay and say: 'Comrades! This can't go on any longer. What shall we do to put an end to these atrocities?'

Then Kirsti raises her fist and shakes it above her head, calling for revenge.

A FEARFUL NOISE IN THE KITCHEN WAKES ME UP, as if an earthquake were shaking the house. Sometimes it's something enormously large collapsing, the hubbub debouching into a horrible crash. Then you hear nothing but a clattering and tinkling, but just when you think it's all come to an end, there are more thumps and bangs, even angrier than before.

Suddenly the door is jerked open and Njanja with Baby in her arms is standing there, wildly and tearfully calling for Aunt: 'Dear Lord! What shall we do? She's wrecking the whole kitchen.'

The racket increases. It's as if sky-high mountains of plates, metal pans, firewood, tables, chairs and cupboards were being piled up and then knocked over. Baby is yelling. Tommy is standing upright in his barred cot, waiting for Aunt to dress him. He's blinking as if about to burst into tears.

'Hurry!' cries Njanja to Aunt, who is buttoning up her skirt. 'She's stark staring mad. Before we know where we are, she'll be sticking a knife into us all.'

At that moment the racket starts in the living-room, too. Someone is shrieking in there in a shrill hoarse voice. It sounds peculiar and alien, not at all like a human being, because no human being would be able to shriek so loudly and angrily for so long. All the time you're expecting the shrieks to blow to pieces and fall silent. But they just go on and on and the words follow on each other so quickly you can't possibly make them out, only the shrieks themselves, which sound like the howls of a monster.

When I look behind Njanja's back into the living-room, I see that it's Kirsti screaming at Grandmother and Mamma. She's wearing her dark blue coat and the black hat with pom-poms on it. Her yellow travelling-box tied round with string is on the floor beside her. Her face is red, her hat crooked, her knot of hair undone, her hair hanging down like a cobweb over her forehead and eyes. 'Butchers!' she is shrieking. 'Bloody butchers!'

She goes over to the table and jerks off the cloth, scattering the paraffin lamp, the coffee-cups and everything else on the table on to the floor. Grandmother is standing in the doorway to her room, not moving, just watching. Mamma is crying and trying to explain something. But Kirsti spits at Mamma, kicks away the shattered lamp and goes up to Grandmother. Her green eyes are glimmering like a tiger's, her face all trembling wrinkles, the veins in her neck swelling. She curls her fingers into claws and the pom-poms on her hat bob and leap. Her teeth are bared, ready to bite.

'We must lock the door,' says Aunt. 'So she can't get in here.'

'Dear Lord!' sighs Njanja. 'This'll be the end of the old lady.'

'Run!' says Aunt. 'Call for help! Run to old Mr Sesemann and ask him to come immediately.'

'But the little one!' sighs Njanja, settling Baby on her arm. She turns down his lace collar and blows something off it. 'I can't leave the little one. She might break in here at any moment and strangle him.'

'But neither can I leave the boys,' says Aunt impatiently. 'Or ... wait. ...' She goes over to the balcony door and opens it a little. The curtains flap and a few snowflakes dance into the room. I can feel the cold welling in and sliding up my bare legs under my night-shirt. 'I'll go this way,' says Aunt, turning round. 'Njanja will stay with you. Get yourselves dressed. I'll be back soon.'

We do as Aunt says. The shrieking goes on beyond the closed door.

'Bloody butcher bitch! Bloodsuckers, your time has come!'

Then the balcony door flies open and slams again with a rattling bang. Aunt is back and standing there, red and gasping, snow on her hair and eyebrows. 'Too late,' she gasps. 'They're already here!'

'Batjuski!' cries Njanja, bursting into tears. She sits down on the floor and crosses herself. 'Lord have mercy on me!'

'Shush, shush, shush! They're coming now!'

Aunt creeps over to the locked door and presses herself against it as if glued there. When we open our mouths to ask why she's doing that, she motions us to be quiet. We hold our breath.

There's a noisy stamping in the hall and we hear the front door creaking and slamming shut again and again, heavy steps echoing through the house which is buzzing with dull growling voices, murmurs and neighing laughter. Now they're already in the living-room. I can hear them tramping round and scraping their paws on the floor. There must a terrible lot of them. They fill the whole room and you can feel the floor quaking, walls creaking and the door Aunt is pressed against bulges in towards us. Someone is walking round the drawing-room thumping on the walls with his fist. His fist must be made of iron, because it sounds like hammer-blows. The whole house is shaking and dust and rubbish rustle down behind the wallpaper.

Then we hear Grandmother speaking to them. She speaks for a long time, her voice subdued and calm so that all you can hear is a monotonous mumble as from a stream. The drawing-room turns absolutely quiet. You can hear them sitting quite still, pricking their ears to hear what Grandmother has to say in her defence. When Grandmother stops, movement and life start up again in the drawing-room. Chair legs scrape and an angry voice asks Grandmother what food there is in the house. Grandmother answers. She speaks for a long time, but the voice interrupts her and demands the keys of the cellar. Grandmother's attempts to divert them by offering them coffee are to no avail. She has to knock on our door and ask Njanja to show them the cellar. But Aunt closes the door so quickly we have no time at all to see into the drawing-room. The whole room was full of bluish smoke and we couldn't even count all of them crowded in there, they were so many. Most of them were as grey as wolves, but there were also some in horrible hairy black fur coats. They looked like bears and buffaloes. Some had moustaches and tusks like walruses, some goatee beards. Gun barrels and bayonets protruded everywhere and they all had bright red armbands.

Aunt doesn't open the door and let us out into the drawing-room until the living-room is empty and the whole house is silent.

The cold and the acrid smell of wild animals they have left behind them strikes you. The floor is covered with lumps of snow and big glass-clear discs of water trembling on the carpet. Grandmother is pattering to and fro in the room with a burning juniper twig in her hand. The needles crackle and the twig glows at the top like an angel feather as it sends out billowing white wisps of smoke. It smells of Christmas and holiness, and soon the smell of wild animals has gone when you draw breath.

But Grandmother is not satisfied. 'Open the windows!' she says, snorting. 'The air's so thick you can hardly breathe. The way that smell clings!'

'Who was it, Grandmother? What did they want?' we ask.

'It was the Reds,' sighs Grandmother. 'A godless rabble. They rob and steal and desecrate the churches. Nothing is sacred to them.'

The kitchen looks terrible. Everything lying all over the place, the floor covered with broken china, smashed soup-bowls, plates and teacups. The china cupboard is open and the shelves are empty. The rubbish pail has been tipped over, a split flour bag is lying on the stove and flour is all over the floor and walls. We look round in horror. Kirsti's revenge is fearful. How shall we ever again be able to cook food and have anything to eat? All the utensils and plates have been destroyed.

'Out of the way,' snaps Aunt, who is down on the floor sorting the rubbish. 'Look, now you've trodden on a saucer and broken it.'

'Where's the bag of sugar?' cries Mamma, searching on the shelves. 'Heavens! Can she really have taken it with her? Our whole ration!'

When you creep up on to the kitchen table, you can see the Reds through the window. There are three sledges on the road outside the front porch. The horses' shafts and reins are decorated with red ribbons and the Reds are sitting in the sledges in hairy caps and black sheepskin jackets. Some of them have homespun coats on, just like ordinary workers, but they've also got red bands on their arms and rifles over their shoulders. Kirsti is standing in front of one of the sledges and the Reds are helping her lift up her box. Then she herself gets into the sledge and sits on her box. One of the Reds puts his arm round her waist and she throws herself backwards and laughs. Then a whole line of them come slowly up from the cellar, all of them carrying something. Last of all comes Njanja. She's walking quite crookedly and keeps wiping her face with her apron.

It's snowing. Great white flakes are swirling like moths through the air. Sometimes they're all falling to the right, then all at once they stand still, dance round, change direction and fly to the left. The swirling snowflakes and the flapping red ribbons give a festive impression. When they've all got up on the sledges, someone starts playing an accordion. The horses set off, someone cheers, throwing up his cap and catching it again. A red flag rises on a wobbly pole and flaps away like a red bird in the whirling snow. Then it's all over and you can see nothing but the empty road and streaks of snow flying past the window.

Njanja is crying when she comes in. 'They took everything,' she sobs. 'The hams, the head, the trotters – they didn't even leave the liver and kidneys behind.'

TERRIBLE THINGS HAVE HAPPENED. SORKKA AND
Palonen the butchers have rebelled against God – just
like Satan once upon a time when he was an angel and
was hurled down from heaven with all his followers. And
it's all a result of Grandmother's cruel and over-eager
decision to slaughter Jonah. For he was a sacred pig and
she should have been able to foresee the misfortunes his
death would evoke.

Now Sorkka and Palonen rule the world. They
fear nothing and do exactly as they please. They have
deposed all the princes and generals, killed Nikolaschka,
his children and all, and like Satan they have had
themselves proclaimed the rulers of the world. The
Reds Mamma and Grandmother are so afraid of are
quite simply Sorkka's and Palonen's henchmen. On
their orders, the Reds seize people and slaughter them
just as if they were pigs. No one's life is safe any
longer.

'The whole world has been turned upside-down,'
says Grandmother. She's probably exaggerating a little,
because here at Teerilä everything is in its place. But over
there beyond the forests, Sorkka and Palonen really have
turned everything upside-down, though only Grandmother can see it. There are beggars and coachmen clad
in silk and velvet, kitchen-maids parading in princess
dresses and cleaning women in sables. Kings are sweeping the streets, countesses cooking in the kitchen, generals serving soldiers, and judges and policemen being
dragged off to prison by thieves and robbers.

114

So it's not at all strange that Mamma and Aunt are so worried and afraid, and that Uncle Georg is so terribly angry. Even here at Teerilä, you can see what Sorkka and Palonen have been up to. It's got so cold, Grandmother has to have a hot-water bottle when she goes to bed. And Njanja has toothache and goes around all the time with a woollen cloth tied round her head so that only the tip of her nose and her mouth show. And the water in the bowl is full of pieces of ice when you're going to wash yourself in the morning. It's their fault butter gets more expensive every day so that Njanja plumps down on the kitchen stool and says 'Lord have mercy on me!' whenever Mamma comes home from Viborg. They're the ones who have tied a red armband round Riika and ordered her to walk to and fro in front of the dairy. And they're the ones who have put Katri the washerwoman in huge hairy felt boots and a rifle over her shoulder on the Viborg road so that no one can get past without asking her permission.

But the Grown-ups are most horrified and angry about Sorkka and Palonen saying no one need obey anyone any longer, and that no one can keep their own things any more. Everyone is to have everything together. Each and every one can go and take a thing from someone else whenever he likes and thinks he needs it. The Grown-ups are afraid the Reds will come and take everything away from us.

The Grown-ups have become nasty and bad-tempered. Mamma always talks in a complaining voice, and as soon as she sees you she maintains you're dis-obedient and you mustn't distress her now when she's got so many troubles and sorrows anyhow. If you don't do what she tells you at once, she starts crying and asks why we have to torment her so.

Aunt is awkward and curt. She wants you to do everything horribly quickly. She snatches things out of your hands, shoves you and pulls your leg when she's lacing your boots and she's always saying that never in her whole life has she seen such dirty lazy children. She always gives the same answer to all your questions: 'Wait! I haven't time now.'

When I've waited for ages and ages and I consider I've waited long enough, so that Aunt will have become nicer and will answer me, she is sitting with a cardboard box in front of her, sorting a whole lot of letters and postcards spread out on the table. Her lips are pursed and her face is quite red, as if she had been standing over a steaming pan. When I cautiously touch her arm, she looks at me as if she doesn't recognize me at all. 'Is it you again?' she snaps suddenly. 'Can't I be left alone for a moment?'

I am not allowed to look at the lovely postcards she is sorting into piles and tying up with blue and pink bits of ribbon. There are pictures of sweet little kittens, smiling ladies with huge bouquets of lilac in their arms, moustachioed gentlemen with shiny cylinders on their heads, and beringed hands squeezing each other. I am allowed to stay with her only on condition I'm as quiet as a mouse.

Nastiest of all is Njanja. You keep hearing her muttering and scolding in the kitchen. She's usually alone when you go into the kitchen and you've no idea with whom she is quarrelling so dreadfully. As soon as she sees you, she shouts and comes waddling over to you with a ladle or a dishcloth in her hand. 'Vot!' she hisses, waving her arm as if chasing off some animal. 'Damned monkeys! Vot! Haven't I told you not to come running around in here!'

She keeps saying we make a mess and clutter everywhere. That we don't brush the snow off our feet when we come in through the kitchen way, and that we dirty the mat in the kitchen porch and bring snow into the kitchen. She's forbidden us to use the kitchen entrance and says we must run round the house and knock on the front door when we want to come in. Once when I'd forgotten to do that, she took the big broom and swept me out through the kitchen door. I ran away as fast as I could, but I tripped over the kitchen mat and she hit my leg so hard with the broom, twigs broke off it and got caught up in my stockings.

Only Grandmother is just the same. But she stays in her room most of the time. You can hear Mamma complaining in there, but Grandmother hardly ever answers. Only in the mornings when Njanja is cleaning does Grandmother sit in the living-room with her cards. The cards are lovely and colourful. There are red and black hearts, squares and crosses, kings with wavy beards, queens with low-cut dresses and princes with feathers in their hats. Now and again Grandmother moves the cards on the table, covering a king with a heart or putting a queen aside, but mostly she sits quite still and just looks at the cards. You mustn't disturb Grandmother. She's looking at the cards to see how the War will go and who will win in the end, God and Kaiser Wilhelm or Satan and his friends Sorkka and Palonen. And Grandmother always looks very worried when she's looking at the cards. She shakes her head at the kings and queens and sighs deeply. Then she puts them all away. 'It didn't come out,' she says to Mamma. 'The Jack of Hearts spoilt it all.'

The Jack of Hearts – that's Sorkka. He wears red velvet and holds a shiny axe in his hand. He has a small cruel mouth and little silky black moustache. Beside him hangs a blood-red heart, as on the wall of a butcher's shop.

THE WORST THING SORKKA AND PALONEN HAVE done here at Teerilä is that Baal the bull has appeared again outside the byre, where he's been shut in all summer.

Recently his bellowing has got worse and worse, and when we walk past the byre, my heart jumps within me every time he bellows inside. I'm glad of the thick stone wall between us. Sometimes you can hear his bellows as far away as on the kitchen balcony. He sounds as if he were mocking Grandmother and was pleased at the confusion out in the world. He's waiting for Sorkka and Palonen to give him back the power he had in the past.

Grandmother doesn't take much notice of him. Once when the living-room was being aired and Bull's bellows were echoing over from the stable buildings, she pulled down the corners of her mouth, snorted scoffingly and asked Aunt to close the window. But that evening she took out the Bible and read: 'We are confounded, because we have heard reproach: shame hath covered our faces. . . .'

She swallowed, took out her handkerchief and blew her nose.

'Wherefore, behold, the days come, saith the Lord, that I will do judgment upon her graven images: and through all her land the wounded shall groan. Though Baal should mount up to heaven, and though she should fortify the height of her strength, yet from me shall spoilers come unto her, saith the Lord.'

Once when we were on our way to the Big House,

we came across a crowd outside the byre. I recognized Ali, Aho-Mikko with his sorrowful drooping Chinese moustaches, and Hämäläinen with his rolling eyes. Katri the washerwoman was there with her rifle on her back, her stomach stuck out, and Riika was leaning on a pole with a red pennant fluttering on the end of it. Some workers' children were looking on, fingers in their mouths. The byre door was open and Bull's rumbling voice was echoing from inside, moaning on monotonously but now and again rising into a menacing bellow. You could see everyone was upset. They kept forgetting to listen and went on shouting at each other and gesticulating as if they simply couldn't agree. After a while Riika handed her pennant over to Aho-Mikko and disappeared into the byre. When she appeared again in the black square of the doorway, she raised her hand to quieten the others down. The men took off their caps and the women clasped their hands. A stranger in a grey soldier's cloak jumped up on a box and waved his hands about. They all began to sing and Bull joined in. His bellows became more and more belligerent the longer they went on.

Aunt stood there for a long time, looking down from the stable bank. 'That they aren't ashamed!' she said at last. She wouldn't go any closer, but said we would make a detour round the stables.

The first time Bull was let out, it all looked very festive. He had a red ribbon round one horn, and as he rushed to and fro outside the byre, the ribbon fluttered like a flame behind him. He bellowed and flung up his tail and back hoofs like a frisky calf. That didn't really suit his awful appearance and huge body, and he just looked silly. Riika and Anna ran after him, laughing their heads off. Some of the workers standing looking on a little way away shouted encouragingly at him and then he behaved even more crazily.

Bull was dancing a war-dance for them. He reared up,

threw himself from one snowdrift to another, as if fighting invisible opponents and vanquishing them one by one. As he dug up the drifts with his front hoofs and horns, the snow swirled round and enveloped him in a cloud of sparkling stars. In the end, when everything round him was trampled to pieces, he threw himself down and rolled back and forth, flinging his hoofs up in the air and bellowing with joy. His vast black and white spotted stomach swayed like a barrel and he rubbed his nose against the crust of snow, then licked it with his long tongue.

We were watching this spectacle from the stable loft, where we had fled to safety. Aunt held the door slightly open so that we could see what was happening down there. We couldn't get down again, because now Bull was just outside the stable steps and at any moment he might rush up them and butt the door down. But he was so occupied prancing about and dancing for the workers, he never noticed us.

After a while we saw Uncle Georg coming lolloping down the stable slope. He was annoyed about the noise and shouted at Riika and Anna. When Bull caught sight of him, he arched his back, pulling his head down between his front hoofs so that his golden ring was touching the ground. You could see he was pleased to be meeting a real flesh-and-blood enemy. Two white columns of smoke rushed hissing out of his nostrils and his tail whipped smartly over his sides. But Uncle Georg had no idea what was going on and again shouted at the girls, shaking his leather glove at them threateningly.

Bull replied with a bellow and started moving in Uncle's direction, at first slowly swinging his head from side to side, but then more and more quickly, like an engine getting up steam. No one tried to stop him or step in between to defend Uncle Georg. On the contrary, Riika and Anna burst out laughing, and the workers shouted as if they wanted to set Bull on Uncle Georg. For a moment, Uncle Georg stayed where he was, lobster-red in the face, his stick above his head as if he were about to crush Bull and the disobedient farm girls with one single blow, then he whirled round and fled up the slope. We could see him hurrying faster and faster, sometimes turning round to look at Bull, who was gradually closing in on Uncle Georg.

The farm men roared with laughter, some of them slapping their knees and squatting down. When Uncle and Bull had disappeared round Simo's cottage, the farm girls at last grabbed their sticks and ran after them to help Uncle Georg, at least for appearance' sake. I thought the end had already come for him, but he popped up on the other side of the cottage with Bull still after him. He was running for his life now, his coat-tails flapping, his back arched and his stomach out as if he could already feel Bull's horns tickling his back. But Bull was in no hurry. He looked as if he couldn't be bothered to try to catch up with Uncle. All he wanted to do at the moment was to pursue him, then all the fun would be over.

As soon as Bull and Uncle Georg had vanished out of sight, Aunt pushed the door open, grabbed our hands and said the way was clear. We rushed home as if we ourselves were being chased by Bull.

The next morning we heard that Bull had chased Uncle Georg three times round the grain store and in the end forced him to climb up the ladder to the safety of the roof of the store. Bull had refused to go back into the byre and had rushed around between the workers' cottages so that they had also been scared. He had pursued Kuri Mari right up to her cottage, so that she had slipped on the steps and sprained her foot. And he had frightened Simo's youngest daughter, little Lyyli, who had opened the porch door just a little, so badly she had the cramps that night. In the end, all the men had to help drive him back into the byre and shut him up in there again.

'THE MICE HAVE BEEN AT IT AGAIN!' SAYS AUNT IN the morning.

The mice haven't eaten all that much, only gnawed at the crust of the rye loaf, so it's covered with pale patches as if it had a rash. Mamma complains and says we must throw away the whole loaf, but Grandmother replies that the loaf will do if we just cut off the crust where the mice have been. She takes the bread knife and shows how it's done.

'They're eating up all our food,' sighs Mamma. 'We'll soon have nothing left.'

'Yes, they're a real plague,' says Grandmother, pushing her glasses straight so that she can see the bread she's holding in her hand better. 'I didn't get a wink of sleep last night.'

It really is true that the mice have become a nuisance. Now that there's no more food out there in the world, they've moved in on us and want us to share our food with them. But the Grown-ups don't want to give them anything. They say we must keep everything for ourselves. So the mice have begun to steal. It's no use Aunt and Njanja finding hiding-places and locking the food up. The mice are more cunning than they are and always succeed in finding out where the hiding-places are. The Grown-ups are terribly annoyed – but really, they're unfair. The mice have to steal to survive.

The mice are usually invisible and silent so you might think they didn't exist at all, but they do that just to deceive us. They're looking at us all the time through cracks in the wall. As soon as they see a room is empty, or that our backs are all turned, they patter soundlessly out of their holes. They snatch up breadcrumbs from under the table, jump up on the seats of chairs and on to the table and sniff in the dishes to find something good.

Once a mouse hid himself under a rusk in the bread basket. Aunt screamed and dropped the basket. I didn't have time to see more than a flash of black lightning disappearing under the piano. A mouse also drowned in the jar of pickled mushrooms and Njanja held it up by its tail before flinging it into the rubbish pail. It looked dreadful, its coat all matted and wet, dripping with vinegar. You couldn't even see its face; only the little pink paws were right. I felt terribly sorry for it although it had been so rash and greedy.

One morning another mouse was so cheeky it crept up on to Grandmother's bed and snatched a sugar lump from her tea-tray. Grandmother picked up the bell from her bedside table and called for help. Mamma and Aunt came rushing in, but the mouse had already gone into hiding, dropping the sugar lump in fright when Grandmother rang the bell so loudly. Grandmother maintained the mouse had hidden in her bed, but it had vanished, although Mamma took the whole bed apart and Aunt crawled underneath to look for it.

But it wasn't just the mice who were hungry. I was hungry, too – terribly hungry. Inside Aunt's drawer, there's half a loaf and a bag of lump sugar. She's hidden them there so the mice won't get at them and steal them. Sometimes when Aunt has her raspberry-leaf tea in the nursery, she takes out the bread and the bag of sugar. She cuts a thin slice off the loaf, takes a sugar lump out of the bag, and then drinks her tea *au canard*. She does it very slowly and quite quietly, as if she is doing something very important. Now and again she puffs and you hear the sugar crunching between her teeth as she bites off a bit. She bites tiny little pieces off the slice of bread and chews them thoroughly for a long time, as if eating a wonderful cake and afraid it will come to an end all too soon. I stand beside her and can't take my eyes off her mouth. The strange thing is that I have to swallow every time Aunt swallows, although I don't want to at all. When Aunt has at last finished, she sighs, takes the loaf and the bag of sugar and hides them again in her drawer. She used to be nice and shared the sugar and bread if you wheedled and begged her to. But now Mamma and Grandmother have told us not to beg for food from Aunt, for the food is *hers* – Mamma and Grandmother see to our food and it is locked inside Grandmother's room.

I wait all day for food and can't think of anything else. It's just as if I were hollow inside. Inside me there's nothing but a gaping space that sucks and sucks and can never be filled. Even when I'm eating, it helps for only a little while – then I get a pain in my stomach and it starts gnawing away under my chest again and I can feel the empty space in there opening out. It makes you so tired and miserable, you can't even be bothered to play. If I try running around and making a noise like I used to, I'm soon so tired I have to sit down or lie on the floor. I'm always cold although I have on a tricot vest as well as a shirt, jerkin and woollen sweater indoors. And if I go out, the wind blows right through me as if I were full of holes like a strainer.

Aunt says I must eat more and stop fussing over my food, otherwise the same thing will happen to me as to Augustus when he wouldn't eat his soup. But then she brings in that horrible brown porridge, all lumps and bits of husk. The husks stick on your tongue, between your teeth and in your throat, so you have to keep spitting and clearing your throat. The bread is so dry and hard, it hurts your teeth when you bite it. We never get any butter. Everything tastes and smells of paraffin. I can taste it as soon as I see the plate Aunt has put in front of me, and then I soon feel full and rather sick. But as soon as she's taken the food out, I'm hungry again.

The only thing that helps is putting my thumb in my mouth and sucking it. Then you become a kind of huge sucking mouth which at last has something to hold on to and the whole of the rest of your body has gone and no longer torments you. You swallow and swallow and feel the way the thumb is sucked in and fills out the empty space inside. It is turned into a huge slice of hot freshly baked rye bread with a thick layer of melting butter on it.

'Sucking your thumb again?' hisses Aunt. 'Just like a baby. Shall I go and fetch Baby's dummy?'

I'm dreadfully ashamed when Aunt catches me sucking my thumb. The worst and most shaming thing in the world is to be like a baby, so you can suck your thumb only in secret. But even then it feels good for only a short while, then your tongue smarts, you dribble down your chin and your thumb just tastes of thumb. The sausages, pies, orange segments and ice-cream cones you've had in your mouth have gone and don't come back, however much you call to them. Instead comes that horrid picture of the tailor flying in through the door with his long scissors to cut off poor Conrad's thumbs. Although you know the tailor is only in a book and not behind the door, you have to take your thumb out of your mouth and wipe it on your woollen shirt.

I have to put everything in my mouth and suck on it, bite it, gnaw it. Sometimes we play that we're rats and gnaw at the arms of the chairs and the table legs. It feels good to open your mouth as wide as you can and feel your teeth sinking into the wood. It smells good and the marks remind me of the decorations on cream cakes and confectionery. But the wood is hard and dry and your teeth and lips ache when you try to bite harder. We can't gnaw it right away and eat it up as the rats and mice do. How wonderful it would be if the tables and chairs – yes, the whole house – were all made of gingerbread so that you could nibble at it like Hansel and Gretel.

THERE'S A GREAT STIR ON IN THE HALL. GRANDMOTHER
is standing there with a galosh in her hand, Mamma, Aunt
and Njanja leaning forward, looking on and shaking their
heads.

'Look at that hole!' Grandmother is saying, pointing
at a spot on the toe where the rubber has been gnawed
away and the grey material is showing.

'I don't understand,' says Mamma. 'The galoshes
have been here under the coat-stand among the overshoes all the time. No one has touched them.'

'But they were all right last time I had them on,' interrupts Grandmother impatiently. 'I went out a week ago.'

'How can Madam think . . .' Aunt begins, her face
turning bright red.

But Njanja interrupts. 'Mouse. Rat. Vot!' She wipes
her glistening red hand on her apron, points at the kitchen
door and tells them. Mamma and Aunt look at each other
and sigh.

'This is really going too far,' says Grandmother.
'This. . . .'

They all start arguing about what ought to be done
about the mice. Njanja tells them of the wicked things
they've done in the kitchen and Aunt says they've been in
the drawer in her chest of drawers at night and stolen her
food rations. They've eaten a great hole in her loaf and torn
the sugar-bag. A lot of the sugar lumps have disappeared.
While Aunt is speaking, I can feel my heart thumping in
my chest. It's thumping so hard it can be heard all over the
room and I creep away in terror.

The nursery is empty and silent. The drawer in Aunt's chest of drawers is tight shut and the keyhole peers slyly and accusingly at me. The armchairs and the cupboard are standing quite still, as if to attention, looking at me with dignified grave expressions as if expecting something special. Everything is holding its breath. I refuse to be frightened, but step calmly into the room, swinging my arms, circle a few times round the rag-rug so that it rucks up, and I even try to whistle, though not very successfully. For a moment I amuse myself by balancing along one of the stripes in the rag-rug over to the door without stepping off, then I go over to the toy box and squat down at a safe distance from the chest of drawers, which is still peering at me with its sly keyhole.

When I turn round, I see something gliding along the skirting-board. At first I think it's the shadow of my hand, because it's moving without the slightest sound. But then I see it's a mouse. It's awfully sweet, with a downy greyish-brown coat, pink fluffy ears and shiny eyes that are looking questioning and frightened. Its nose and tail tremble all the time as it nips to and fro sniffing at the floorboards. Suddenly it sits up, looks straight into my eyes and holds its forepaws up as if begging. Its nose and upper lip twitch as if it wanted to say something. Then it starts and shoots off like a dark streak into the wall. Before I can blink, it has gone, as if it had never been there and I'd imagined everything. Why was it so frightened? I was holding my breath all the time, trying to look really friendly.

I lie face down in front of the hole and try to look inside it, but it's pitch-dark and silent in there. It's a pity I can't make myself so small by magic that I could go down into the hole in the wall and explain everything.

That afternoon, Uncle Georg comes into the drawing-room. He looks grim and has a black leather case in his hand. He puts it down on a chair, takes off his glasses and polishes them for ages with his handkerchief. 'Now let's see,' he says. 'The traps should be in order.'

He opens his case and lines up a number of peculiar contraptions on the table. He fingers them, then puts them down – and at once the traps snap shut and take a great leap, just as if they were alive.

Mamma says the traps are much too dangerous and could cut the fingers off us children. But Uncle Georg replies that we can be given a good hiding, then no doubt we'll be careful. He looks at me and bursts into a great rumbling laugh. I retreat in terror towards the nursery door, for you never quite know whether Uncle Georg is joking or whether he means it.

'Have you got any cheese rind or pork crackling?' he says.

'What are you talking about!' cries Mamma. 'We haven't seen anything like that for months.'

Uncle Georg has to be content with bread crusts. The Grown-ups go round the house, pushing aside furniture and looking for mouseholes. They put traps everywhere. In the nursery beside Aunt's chest of drawers Uncle Georg puts a big trap like a cage. When everything's ready, he turns with his rumbling laugh to Grandmother, who has followed him to the door.

'I assure you, Muscha, after three days there won't be a living mouse here, and you'll be able to sleep like the Sleeping Beauty. If anyone knows about catching mice, then it's me!'

I think Uncle Georg is silly boasting like that. He's gone on in that loud voice all the time and of course the rats and mice will have heard every word. How would they allow themselves now to be deceived into nibbling at those crusts? The only reason would be that they were so hungry that they went and ate the bread although they knew it would cost them their lives. But can anyone really be that greedy?

When I'm on my own with Aunt – Bernt and Tommy have gone to say good-night to Mamma – she at once says: 'I suppose you haven't by any chance been in my drawer and eaten some of my sugar and bread?'

She says it like that, as if in passing, without looking at me, as she is pouring water into the basin, just as if she meant nothing by saying it. I hold my breath and am quite silent. Aunt doesn't say anything either, but puts the jug aside and feels with her finger to see if the water is too cold. Her face is friendly and you can't tell whether she knows anything or is just pretending or whether in fact she knows nothing at all.

'No,' I say when the silence begins to be painful. 'What do you mean?'

Aunt looks at me and I raise my eyes and look straight into hers. If only it were over and Aunt had turned her eyes away.

'I haven't touched your drawer,' I say.

'Well, that's good,' says Aunt. 'I thought. . . .'

At last she looks away, reaching out for the washing glove, pulling it over her hand and dipping it into the water. The whole thing hadn't been as bad as I'd thought. So I say: 'It's not me. It's the mice who've stolen your food.'

'Do you think so?' says Aunt. 'I can't think how they manage to get inside the drawer when it's closed.'

'I saw them myself going in to steal. Today, when I was alone in here, a little mouse came out of a hole in the wall and was about to creep up to the chest of drawers to go stealing. But when it saw me it was so frightened, it soon nipped back into the wall again.

'And another time,' I go on, surer now that Aunt is listening and not contradicting me. 'Another time, a great fat rat crept right under the chest of drawers with a sugar lump in its mouth.'

'You're not fibbing, are you?' Aunt says, interrupting me, suddenly looking at me rather strangely.

'I'm not lying!' I cry indignantly. 'I can show you the hole in the wall.'

Aunt lifts up my chin so that I have to meet her gaze. I mustn't be afraid of her eyes at this moment. I must think about that little mouse – the way it sat up and looked at me with its dark eyes and how its nose and upper lip twitched. I know I've seen it and so it's Aunt and not me lying if she says the mouse doesn't exist. And all the rest's also true. I can see that horrid rat coming out, sucking on Aunt's sugar lump. She's sucking so greedily, her cheeks are quite hollow and, when the sugar lump is finally eaten up, she carefully licks her forepaws and pats her tight stomach with contentment. It's the mice and the rats who've eaten Aunt's food and not me.

'I trust you,' says Aunt. 'You've never lied to me before. Come now, so that I can wash you.'

She knows nothing! I think as I stand leaning over the basin with my eyes tight shut and Aunt's hand in the washing glove rubs the back of my neck. She can never find out about *that* if I always think about the mice and not. . . .

I can't sleep, although Aunt has blown out the lamp and wished us good-night. The mice are noisy inside the wall. They creep and mince about and scratch, sometimes swooping up and down the wall as if they were flying. I stiffen with fright, because it sounds exactly like a ghost. Sometimes they go quite wild, thumping and leaping and dancing round in a ring up there and the ceiling paper rustles as if it were hailing. In between, they squeal and whistle to frighten me really properly. But they mostly just gnaw because they're so terribly hungry. They eat up the planks, the beams, the tiles, the nails – they're eating up the whole house from the inside. The walls, the ceiling and the floors are probably already hollow and it's amazing the house still holds together at all. When I turn over on my back and listen, I can hear the sound of innumerable crunching teeth in the darkness around me – sometimes closer, sometimes further away. I can see them in front of me as they hang down the walls, packed tight like ants in an ant-heap. My stomach contracts when I listen to those small nibbling teeth eating their way into the wood. I have to put my thumb in my mouth and suck very hard for a long time. Then I'm no longer afraid and the pain in my stomach gradually goes away.

I KNOW IT'S MORNING, BUT I DON'T WANT TO WAKE
up yet, so keep my eyes shut and press my face into the
pillow. It's nice and warm in bed. If only you could
always lie like this and never have to throw off the
covers, or put your feet on the cold floor and go over
to the bucket to pee! The others are already awake. I
can hear the door opening and closing, the floorboards
bouncing up and down under Aunt's feet, the bits of ice
tinkling as she pours water into the basin. Bernt's bare
feet patter across the floor and it gurgles like a stream
when he pees. Why does he have to pee for so long and
disturb me? When will he stop so that I can at last go back
to sleep? I pull the covers over my head and curl up. The
sounds around me are dulled and distant and I can feel
myself slowly sinking back to sleep.

But a cry from Bernt at once means I'm wide awake.
I open my eyes and sit up in bed.

'Aunt! Aunt! A mouse! Look, a little mouse is inside
the trap!'

Bernt is standing in the corner in his night-shirt,
holding up the trap Uncle Georg had put there the day
before. You can just see something small and black
behind the wire, nervously rushing to and fro, gliding
up the wires and disappearing. Bernt is smiling as he
looks into the trap. 'Look, Riki,' he says, coming over to
my bed. 'Look what sweet ears it has and the funny way
it moves its tail.'

When I put my face close to the trap, the mouse
rushes over the other side in terror and presses itself

against the wire. You can't see its feet. It's like a ball of
greyish brown fluff with a shiny black eye and a long thin
tail at the back. The little mouse is terribly frightened,
shaking from its nose to the tip of its tail and refusing to
sit still for a moment so I can take a proper look at it. It
should have realized ages ago that it would never be able
to get out of the cage on its own, but it still rushes round
trying to stick its nose through the wire as if hoping at
last to find a hole to slink out through. Then it sits up –
its stomach is white and fluffy and it holds up its paws as
if begging, its nose and lip twitching, its eyes glistening
moistly. It wants to cry out to us: 'Why are you doing this
to me? Don't be nasty. Let me out!'

But it can't make a sound. It's that little mouse of
yesterday. Now Aunt can see it with her own eyes and
can no longer doubt my word. I feel terribly sorry for it.
Why on earth was it so rash and greedy? It should have
obeyed its mother, who would be sure to have warned it
about Uncle Georg's stratagem. It wasn't my fault it was
in such a fix now.

'Can't we open the trap and let it out?' I say.

'What are you saying?' says Aunt. 'It would dash
straight back into the wall. And then it'd go on stealing
bread and sugar from my drawer.'

'But it's still so small. Look how sad its eyes are.'

'But it's a thief, all the same. If things were different
we might be able to let the poor thing live. But now when
there's such a shortage of food, we really can't afford to
feed vermin.'

'Don't be childish,' says Bernt. 'Why put out traps if
you're going to let the mice go again?'

Aunt takes the trap and hurries over to the door.

'Where are you taking it?' I cry out in alarm.

'To the kitchen. Njanja will see to it. Perhaps we can
take the trap with us later on in the day and let the mouse
out in the forest on our walk.'

How far is Aunt thinking of carrying the trap? To the
border, where the Russian soldiers have dug trenches? Or

even further away, where the Saarela road branches off? Just think how pleased the little mouse will be when we open the trap and it jumps out into the snow and can rush around as much as it likes. As long as it finds its way out of the forest and doesn't freeze to death. It can never come back here again. It's alone, driven out, and will never see its mother again.

When we were dressed and we ran into the drawing-room to tell Mamma and Grandmother about the little mouse, Njanja was in the hall with a duster in one hand and holding up something else in the other. 'Vot!' she says, smiling contentedly, and her wrinkled red face is glowing. 'Horoscho!'

It's one of those flat traps like a piece of boarding. The wood is blood-stained and something grey and oblong is hanging from it. When I go closer I see that it's a dead rat, its head caught flat on the wood by a loop of brass wire that's almost cut the head off at the neck. Its eyes are tight shut and teeth bared as if it were squealing. Grandmother jerks her face sideways and waves her hand. 'Ugh!' she cries, screwing up her face as if she had just swallowed some quinine. 'Not so close, Marfa Nikolajevna! Take it out into the kitchen. I told you I'd already seen it.'

I follow Njanja out into the kitchen and watch while she takes the rat out of the trap and throws it into the rubbish pail. There are already some mice and rats lying there, not moving, with bloody noses and helplessly holding up those pink curled-up paws that look so like human hands. I can hear them complaining: 'Oh, Lordy me! How horribly we've been betrayed, tortured and murdered! You've strangled us, executed us, drowned us, crushed us under your heels like the worst criminals in the world. And all we wanted was a few crusts of your bread, a few crumbs of your sugar, because we're just as hungry as you are. But quiet, quiet, Riki, say nothing. The end has come and you can't help us anyhow. Now we're here in the rubbish pail, waiting. Soon they'll take us out into the snow and bury us out there in the rubbish dump.'

I suddenly think that the smallest mouse looks familiar. I look up and catch sight of the trap Aunt had taken out into the kitchen. It's there on the kitchen table, empty, the little wire door open. Appalled, I reach down into the rubbish pail and take out the mouse. It's wet and cold, its coat dripping, and it's just as matted and ugly as that stupid mouse which drowned in the jar of pickled mushrooms.

'Where's the little mouse?' I say, looking sternly at Njanja.

'What mouse?' she growls, without turning round.

'The little mouse Aunt brought out into the kitchen. The mouse in the trap.'

'Oh, that one.' Njanja doesn't even bother to answer. She bends down to shove a log into the stove. Sparks fly and a whole lot of glowing charcoal falls to the floor.

'You've killed the little mouse!' I shriek, and I try to open my eyes as wide as possible so that Njanja will be frightened and confess to what she's done.

'Hah!' says Njanja, turning round. 'As if drowning a little mouse mattered. The world's full of mice.'

'How could you?' I can feel the tears coming. 'We were going to take the little mouse a long way away and let it out in the forest. Aunt promised.'

'I know nothing about that,' puffs Njanja, picking up the glowing charcoal and throwing it into the fire, just as if it were the most natural thing in the world and the fire couldn't get the better of her. 'All I know is that mice are vermin. And all vermin in the world should be got rid of.'

'No!' I shriek, bursting into tears. 'You're lying. All mice aren't vermin. That little mouse was a nice mouse. It had never. . . .'

But by now Njanja is really angry. 'Get out of here!' she shouts, reaching out for the fire-tongs. 'Throw that vermin back in the pail and don't make a mess. What do you mean by coming here with all your cheek and blubbing in my kitchen? Vot!'

While we're waiting for breakfast and Aunt is laying the table, I play at being a crocodile. The dining-room floor is the great grey-green, greasy Limpopo River and the cushion on Grandmother's armchair is a nasty old elephant-njanja. I swim over to the armchair and with a roar drag the njanja off the seat, clamping my teeth round the scruff of her neck and then creeping under the sofa where a deep dark cave opens out in the rock. 'Haha!' I mumble, chewing on the elephant-njanja's neck and noticing with pleasure that my voice sounds dull and horrible as I press my nose into the cushion. 'Haha! Do you want to know what I'm going to have for my breakfast today? Can you guess now?' And I growl over and over again so that the old elephant-njanja is really frightened.

But as I crawl deeper into the cave, feeling my way ahead with my hand, something terrible happens. Something goes bang and gives me a stinging rap over my fingers.

Then I'm standing in the middle of the living-room floor. When I try to see what's left of my fingers, I notice that they're caught firmly in a trap. I pull at the trap to free them, but every pull makes it tighten its wire jaws even more and hurts worse than ever. I try running away, but the trap sticks to my hand and comes with me. Then I gather all my strength, draw a deep breath and scream as loudly as I can.

'Stand still!' says Aunt, who has rushed in. 'Wait! Hold up your hand! Not like that.'

It at once hurts less when Aunt is there with me and I'm no longer afraid of the trap at all. And yet I jump and stamp with rage when she doesn't manage to free my hand straight away.

'Don't make such a terrible noise,' says Aunt, taking my hand. She looks at it and blows on my fingers. 'Not so bad after all. Does it really hurt that much?'

I take my hand back and look at it. Goodness, my fingers are still there – the trap didn't bite them right off. My fingertips are a little red and a white line runs right across my knuckles, but I can't see any blood. I can clench my fist perfectly well. But a dull grinding ache is still there and Aunt has no right to say that. She ought to know immediately that it was really all her fault. Instead she reminds me that Uncle Georg told us not to go anywhere near the traps and she scolds me for not looking what I was doing when I was creeping under the sofa. So I just give her a long cross look and go on snivelling.

'Come now, let's go and show Grandmother your hand,' says Aunt.

But there's a terrific fuss going on in Grandmother's room. Grandmother is sitting in her armchair with a galosh in her hand, Tommy in front of her, his face tear-stained. He's quite black round his mouth as if he's been eating dirt, and he's got grey streaks on his cheeks and chin. He's frightened and wants to run away, but Mamma is holding his arm.

'How many times have I told you that you mustn't put things that have been on the floor into your mouth?' says Grandmother. 'You're not a rat. Just look what you've done to my new galosh!'

'You mustn't eat dirty things,' adds Mamma. 'Galoshes are terribly dirty. That could make you ill.'

Tommy wails and jerks his arm in despair, trying to get free.

'Shame on you!' says Grandmother. 'Now you just go and stand in the corner.'

So it wasn't rats which had chewed that large hole in Grandmother's galosh at all. Tommy had secretly crept down into the corner behind the coat-stand and eaten bits off it day after day, without anyone knowing. But today, when Mamma went out into the hall to put her coat on, she had caught him at it.

'Everything comes to light sooner or later,' says Grandmother, looking sternly at Tommy. 'You're quite wrong if you think you can be disobedient when no one is looking. God sees everything and reveals the truth in the end.'

In the middle of the night a terrible noise wakes me up, a screeching like a saw – so loud and close that I hold my breath. Someone wants to come in, dying of hunger and rage. His teeth must be as long and sharp as chisels and are working like a machine. I can hear them splintering the wood as they sink into it, cutting off slivers and inch by inch boring their way through the timber. Sometimes they whine like a grindstone and set my teeth on edge. Sometimes the sound is dull and hollow as from a mill. Then it stops – but only for a moment. He pauses only for a moment to get his breath back and swallow the splinters before he again clamps his teeth round the timber.

'Aunt! Aunt!' I whimper. 'Wake up! Can't you hear?'

Aunt turns over in bed, a match flares and the shadows dance over the walls.

'Sh! Sh! Don't wake the others. What's the matter now?'

'Inside there, in the wall – can't you hear, Aunt?'

Aunt listens, but it's quite quiet, the only sound the even rustle of the wind.

'It's nothing,' says Aunt, yawning. 'You were only dreaming. Go to sleep now.'

'But I can't go to sleep,' I whisper. 'Something's gnawing so terribly.'

Aunt takes her shoe, comes over to my bed and thumps the wall with the heel. 'I expect it's a rat,' she says, turning out the light.

It's hardly dark before the screeching is back again. Sometimes it sounds as if the teeth have already cut through the wall and are gnawing at my bed. I pull my legs up and curl up so that they can't come and cut off my toes.

THE PARK IN SALMELA IS SILENT AND GHOSTLY,
everything in grey and white, the white branches scarcely
visible against the cloudy sky. The lattice-work of rose
bushes is like lace flounces and all the small bushes are
clad in white cotton-wool capes and fur caps that have
slid over their faces. All that white makes your eyes ache.
It's like an optical illusion – if you blew hard the whole
park would whirl away like a dandelion head.

Slowly we make our way up the main avenue to the
house. The road is snowed up, the kick-sledge's runners
sinking deep into the snow and leaving two deep, knife-
sharp incisions behind them. Bernt is panting, because
it's hard work pushing the sledge, and I follow behind
him, trying to step into his tracks.

Suddenly we stop. A branch is swaying up and
down. Two birds with blood-red breasts are clinging
on to it, pecking at some berries. They're red, too, and
the snow scattered on the berries looks like grains of
sugar. The birds are eating quite silently, turning their
little heads hither and thither with delight, their tails
whipping as they keep swinging up and down to get at
the berries more easily.

Bernt signals to me to be quiet. I hold my breath
and try to stand still without blinking. The red birds,
the silvery branch and the snowy park behind it – it's all
so beautiful, you can't really believe it's true. The birds
are pecking swiftly and silently as if they were in a very
great hurry. They must be terribly hungry, because they
don't even notice us standing right beside them. But I'm

also terribly hungry and my mouth waters as I watch the birds eating. It's difficult just standing still looking on, and in the end I can't keep it up and breathe out heavily. 'Look!' I whisper. 'They're eating up all the berries.'

Bernt turns round crossly, but it's already too late, the birds have gone as if they'd never been there. The branch bounces slowly back and forth, sending a swirl of glittering snow to the ground.

We go up to the bush and pick some berries. They are bitter and sour and full of horrid seeds, and they're so small you don't even notice you've eaten anything.

The palace-like building is white like everything else, thick layers of snow on the roof and only the spire on the tower shining as red as the birds and the berries. When we get closer, it is as silent and empty in the courtyard as in the park, just as if everything were bewitched and sound asleep. The house is embedded in snowdrifts and the trees spin a network of white stitches all round it. Glittering icicles hang from the guttering and the window-sills are thick with snow, the panes covered with ice so that you can't see in.

We climb the steps and Bernt bangs on the door. But everything remains silent. We wait for a moment, then Bernt thumps again. He presses the bell and we can hear something rattling inside.

'Don't ring so hard,' I say. 'The aunts might be angry.'

But Bernt presses the bell again. A door slams somewhere and we think we can hear steps inside and expect the door to open any minute to let us in. But nothing happens and everything is just as before.

'They're not at home,' I say, because I'm getting scared. 'Let's go home.'

'Silly!' says Bernt, pressing the bell again. 'Mamma said it was important. . . .'

A shadow suddenly glides across the door's icy pane and a voice croaks impatiently. 'Kukka seele?' it says in a weird sort of Finnish. 'Who there?'

'It's us, Aunt Louise!' we cry. 'Bernt and Riki.'

But the shadow doesn't move.

'Pois! Go away! Huligani! Robbers! Hooligans!'

'But it's us!' we shout as loudly as we can. 'Bernt and Riki. Mamma said . . .'

'You won't get in!' croaks the voice in reply. 'I reports you to General Derleff. I telephones General Posjarski. Vot! General shoots thieves. That's enough! Go away.'

In the end, they at last understand inside. The shadow of a hand becomes visible behind the pane and scratches at the ice on the glass. There's a lot of whispering and shushing. Then the lock clicks, the door is opened very slightly and Aunt Louise's crumpled face peers suspiciously out through the crack. 'You're right, Malla, it really is the children from Teerilä,' she says, and lets us in.

But she soon slams the door again, turning the key and replacing the safety-chain. It's difficult to recognize the aunts, they are so wrapped up. Aunt Louise is wearing a sheepskin jacket with gold buttons and epaulettes, a woollen stocking on her head. And Aunt Malla has thick felt boots on, a padded silk quilt round her shoulders and she nods at us like a wise old Indian chieftain.

'Hurry, hurry!' croaks Aunt Louise, waving the empty sleeves of her sheepskin jacket like a couple of fins. 'So we don't let in any of this awful cold.'

As I'm taking off my outdoor clothes in the hall, the bandage on my hand comes undone and gets caught up in my coat sleeve and buttons. I can hear steps. Someone's coming into the hall and is standing beside me. It's Oliver, and I can feel my cheeks and ears going hot. But he doesn't ask about my chilblains, just puts his hand on the back of my neck and squeezes it in a friendly way.

The drawing-room is dark and as shadowy as a primeval forest. Palm leaves shimmer in the iced-over windows and cross over each other up in the semi-darkness like a vaulted church ceiling. There are flower-pots everywhere on little stands, so you have to walk carefully to avoid bumping into them. Small trees with white flowers grow in the corners, and bundles of soft hanging creepers hide the furniture and shimmer like Christmas-tree glitter. There's a smell of summer so that you almost forget the winter and the cold out there. But Aunt Louise is not pleased. She shivers and pulls the woollen stocking over her ears and says she's never ever experienced such cold indoors before.

Under a myrtle bush on a white marble slab, Popotjka sits enthroned in his cage. He is in a terribly bad temper and can't sit still for a minute. Round and round he climbs on his bars, biting at them as if he were going to gnaw at them with his curved black beak. The sight of us makes him simply furious. All you can see is flapping wings and white down swirling around in the cage. His screams are so shrill and angry, I start back. It would be awful if he managed to smash up his cage and peck out all our eyes.

'Popotjka, dear!' sighs Aunt Louise. 'My dear little dovey-dear. It really isn't my fault.' She digs in her coat pocket and strews a pinch of oats into his feeding-bowl. 'Try to eat a little. Nowadays you have to get used to everything. There now, Popotjka, there now.'

Popotjka quietens down and hops on to the floor of the cage. He picks a seed out of the bowl, chews on it for a moment, smacks with his tongue, but then spits it out again. Then he flaps up on to the steel ring that swings in the middle of his cage, turns his head away and glares thoughtfully at Aunt Louise with his round eye.

'There now, Popotjka,' complains Aunt Louise. 'Be sensible. You're a silly old thing. You know that. Show me now that you're a good boy. Say Popotjka's a silly old parrot. Popotjka durak!'

But Popotjka refuses to speak Russian, however much Aunt Louise begs and implores. He defiantly says nothing and goes on swinging back and forth in his ring. In the end he fluffs himself into a ball, opens his beak and says a few words in a perfectly clear and human voice. I don't understand what he's saying – I don't even know what language he's speaking – but the words clearly mean something quite terrible.

The aunts' faces stiffen and turn pale. Aunt Malla's eyebrows soar up into her forehead. Aunt Louise takes a little leap, trembling with resentment. 'Take the children out, Malla!' she cries. 'Supposing. . . .'

She rushes up to the cage, waving her arms to frighten Popotjka properly, the sheepskin sleeves flapping.

'Quiet, Popotjka! Quiet! At once! In my house. Ssh, ssh, ssch!'

I haven't time to catch anything else, because Aunt Malla takes us out of the drawing-room and closes the door behind her, Popotjka's piercing shrieks and Aunt Louise's croaks echoing behind us, relieving each other at a faster and faster rate and getting louder and louder all the time.

'Why does Aunt Louise do that? What did Popotjka say?' I ask, because I would very much like to find out what those terrible words were that caused such a fuss. But Aunt Malla doesn't answer and Bernt pinches my arm so hard I don't dare repeat the question.

We go into Aunt Malla's room, where it's warmer and lighter, and tall cacti crowd together as in a greenhouse. Aunt Malla leads us over to a heap of clothes by the couch and tells us to say how do you do. At first I don't understand at all, but then the shawls, rugs and cushions begin to move, the springs creak and a bit of Aunt Gulla's face becomes visible under an embroidered table-cloth.

'Oh, children dear,' she gasps, holding out a shaggy woollen glove. 'How nice. So Muscha and Anni are still alive, are they? Give them something hot to drink, Malla. They're sure to have got cold.'

We sit down and Aunt Malla takes out the teacups. I hadn't felt it all that much outside, but now that my fingers were beginning to thaw out indoors, that dull grinding ache which plagues my life comes back again. My knuckles itch and sting so much I don't know what to do with my hands, and the tips of my fingers ache as if they were still squashed in that horrible rat-trap I got caught in. The pain is so bad, tears come into my eyes and blur my sight. The bandage Grandmother put on in the morning came away as I took off my glove and is dangling in ugly dirty loops on my hand. I secretly try to put the bandage right, covering the bad hand with the other one and squeezing the fingers, because then at least it feels better. But although I try in every way to stop the aunts and Oliver from seeing anything, they nevertheless notice. Aunt Gulla wonders if I want to go and pee and Aunt Malla asks me if I've cut myself.

'He's got chilblains,' Bernt tells them obligingly.

I try to hide my hand behind my back, but Aunt Malla seizes it and unwinds the bandage. An ugly yellow patch appears on the bandage and gets larger and larger with every turn. In the middle of the knuckle of my swollen forefinger is a round hole, something slimy and yellowish-green looking out of it like a green worm.

I squeeze my eyes shut because I'm afraid and I'm ashamed about Oliver standing beside me and looking on. Will Aunt Malla also now start squeezing my chilblains like Grandmother does every morning and asking whether it hurts, although she knows perfectly well it does? Isn't it enough that she makes me stand here showing everyone how hideous my hand is?

'Poor boy!' says Aunt Malla. 'Does it hurt badly?'

She takes my sick hand between her cupped palms and blows on it. The ache soon eases. I burst into tears and no longer care what Oliver and Bernt think about it. When I've stopped crying, Aunt Malla has seen to my hand and the ache has almost gone. She gets a new dazzling white bandage out of a drawer and puts it on. Then she pats me on the cheek and says my hand will probably soon be better. When I look back at her slightly distrustfully and self-consciously – because that's what Grandmother usually says every morning and my hand just gets worse

– she hands me a pair of small leather mittens. They have handsome wide cuffs that go a long way up my jacket sleeve and a rim of white fur round the edges. It feels wonderfully warm and soft on the fingers when I put them on, just as if I'd put my hands into a pile of down. I'm terribly pleased when Aunt Malla says I can keep them on and they're mine from now onwards. Bernt looks rather envious, but Oliver smiles in a friendly way and says: 'They're my old mittens, I'll have you know. I had them when I was small.'

My hand feels almost better already inside the mitten.

Aunt Louise comes back from the drawing-room and looks quite exhausted after her quarrel with Popotjka. She carefully closes the door, puts her finger to her lips and shuffles slowly over to us in her hairy black overshoes. She jumps with fright when Aunt Malla closes the drawer with a bang after fiddling around inside it. With a secretive look on her face, she whispers: 'I told you so. It's her. That Donna!'

Who is Donna? Is that Don Juan's sister or the daughter of the statue which took Don Juan to hell with him? In any case, she's dangerous and nasty and it must be terrible to have such a creature in your home. Aunt Louise tells us that Donna has secretly eaten up the last bag of peanuts and all the packets of birdseed. Poor Popotjka! And the other day Donna growled and snapped so horribly that now Aunt Louise doesn't dare go out into the kitchen to ask her to light the samovar.

'Who is Donna?' I finally ask.

'Ssh! Ssh!' hisses Aunt Louise, waving her hands about as if I'd said something terrible. 'Can't you be quiet?'

She turns round with fright and after a while says in a subdued whisper: 'She listens at the doors. Then she goes and tells everything to them out there. We must be careful. Oliver, could you go and see if. . . .'

But there's no one behind the door. Clearly Donna can make herself as invisible as a ghost and lie in wait for us without our knowing.

Before Oliver has had time to get back from the door and managed to get the chair under himself, something awful happens. Someone bangs on the window-pane. First once, then again, really hard and impatiently.

Aunt Louise jumps in her chair and stops in the middle of a sentence. Someone is outside the window wanting to come in, but we can't see him, for the whole window is covered with glittering ice.

'Bandits!' hisses Aunt Louise, seizing a table-knife. We all sit in silence.

'Is it that Donna?' I whisper.

But then there's another knock, even harder, so the whole pane resounds and sings.

But Oliver suddenly bursts out laughing. 'It's the birds!' he cries. 'Can't you see. . . .'

The aunts look at each other with wide-open eyes and raised eyebrows. Then Aunt Gulla also starts laughing so that the rugs and shawls jump and leap about on her stomach.

'Thank goodness,' sighs Aunt Louise, putting the knife down.

'I thought . . .'

'What birds?' we ask, rushing over to the window.

'The little birds,' says Aunt Malla, nodding in confirmation in time with the words. 'The poor little birds. All the food in the forest and in the fields is finished and they've nothing to eat.'

We can hear the little birds outside now. We can hear them fluttering and chattering and see their shadows sliding across the window-pane.

'At first it was just a starving little great tit,' Aunt Malla tells us. 'One morning he was banging on the window and squeaking so miserably, begging for food. The way he pecked and ate when I crumbled up a rusk and scattered the crumbs in the snow! Then he flew away and told all his friends about it. After breakfast the window-sill was full of birds fluttering and hammering on the window with their beaks. More of them come every day. Oliver has made a little house for them.'

'Do you want to see?' says Oliver. He pushes me over to the window, leans over me and blows on the window-pane. The ice melts under his breath, and soon there's a little window in the frosty curtain. The little bird-house appears with its flat roof and four corner supports just beyond the window. Inside the house and up on its roof there's a throng of little birds, pecking and hopping, pushing and shoving, and then they are off like lightning. Then they're back again without your knowing how it's happened. The most wonderful thing of all is that they're so terribly close, just like a picture in a bird-book. I can see the patterns of their wing feathers, the down under their seesawing tails, their velvety black hoods and shiny eyes inquisitively glancing hither and thither. I could stretch out my hand and touch them if the window weren't in the way.

The only thing I don't like is that the birds can never agree with each other but quarrel over the food like really nasty children. They push and shove and try to grab the crumbs out of each other's beaks. A sparrow and a great tit start squabbling over a tiny crumb. They bounce around on the roof of the bird-house like two ruffled balls of feathers, pecking at each other so that down swirls all round them. A little greenish-yellow bird nips the crumb from right under their noses and whirls away. All the birds start chattering and the whole flock rises to chase after the thief.

Suddenly there's a flash like a sunspot. A little bird with red, white, yellow and black patterns on it hunches up on the roof. He's as beautiful as a humming-bird and I call to Oliver and Bernt to come and look. But the other birds begin to chatter so angrily when they see him, he flies away in terror without getting anything to eat. I wait in vain for him to come back. The other birds are probably so nasty because their feathers aren't as beautiful as his. I get so cross, I bang on the window with my fist and shout: 'Shoo! You mustn't be so mean and envious.'

There's a tremendous twittering and chattering outside and the whole flock rises. The bird-house hangs there empty and silent, the half-emptied food-bowl and oats strewn all over the floor – but there's no sign of the beautiful bird.

'What are you doing?' says Oliver, leaning over me. 'You mustn't be nasty and frighten the birds.'

'The birds are nasty themselves. They just fight. They've just chased off a lovely bird so that he got nothing to eat.'

'When there's war and famine,' says Oliver, 'everyone just thinks of himself and no one else.'

'But the lovely bird wasn't like that. And so he went without. He'll starve to death.'

But Oliver smiles confidently and replies: 'None of them will starve to death. They'll all get enough. Do you want to see. . . .'

Aunt Malla hands him a bag of crumbs. He opens the window, pours the crumbs into the bowl and puts it back into the bird-house. Then he leans out, purses his mouth and whistles like a bird. The next moment the window is one great cloud of birds. They swirl past like dazzling streaks and dive down behind Oliver's shoulders. They're not at all afraid of him but flutter around his head, pecking at his hands and twittering and chattering all at once. He answers by twittering and whistling just like them. Sometimes he looks at me and laughs, for some of the birds like him so much they perch on his shoulder and he has to chase them off to stop them flying into the room.

It's great fun to watch, because it really is true that they all have enough and the crumbs are enough for them all. Even the lovely little bird comes back. Oliver whistles to him, holds out his hand and chases away his mean and envious brothers. The little bird flutters for a moment above Oliver's palm and pecks out of it as if out of a bowl.

Then we have to shut the window. Aunt Malla is worried about her cacti and Aunt Louise shrieks that we mustn't let the house get cold so that we all freeze to death. The water in the samovar has at last begun to boil and Aunt Malla has put hot cranberry juice and wheaten crusts on the table.

When we've sat down, I tug at Oliver's arm.

'Can you speak bird-language? Do you understand what the birds are saying?'

'Nearly everything,' he says. 'Didn't you hear me talking to them?'

'Will you teach me it?' I ask him. But Oliver doesn't answer. He smiles mischievously and looks over towards the window. The condensation on the window-pane has obliterated the contours of the bird-house and the birds can just be seen out there as misty spots of colour. You can hear them still twittering and calling to Oliver.

WE RACE OFF HOME, ME SITTING ON THE KICK-sledge and Bernt scooting behind. Underneath me I can feel the firm rounded surface of a sack placed across the seat of the kick-sledge and covered with a blanket.

Just before we left, Oliver and Bernt had come into the hall, followed by Aunt Louise carrying the sack. It was white and looked like a pig as they put it down on the floor. There's something dangerous about that sack. You can't sit comfortably on it. It's hard and heavy but slowly gives way under your weight. You can feel something running away under your backside when you shift position. Aunt Louise kept shushing and sent Aunt Malla to see whether that Donna was listening somewhere. Aunt Malla then kept watch over by the drawing-room door while Oliver and Bernt carried the sack through the hall.

'Ssh! Ssh!' Aunt Louise hissed at me as we went down the steps. 'Don't clump like that. Haven't you ever learnt to walk quietly?'

After they'd put the sack on the kick-sledge, covered it up and I had got up on to the sack, Aunt Louise wrapped another blanket round me and said commandingly: 'Sit still! And remember, don't get up, and say nothing if you meet anyone on the way.' Then she turned to Bernt: 'If anyone asks, say that Riki is ill and has been to the doctor.'

We've now got down to the shore and in front of us stretches a dead straight road with high drifts on each side. It runs straight across the lake, and the ice under the snow is quite black. As we glide out on to it, it starts singing behind us, just as if we were being pursued, although I can't see anything at all when I turn round.

I think of all the awful stories the aunts have told about Sorkka's and Palonen's ill-deeds at Salmela, the way they've taken away loads of hay and corn, so the horses have nothing to eat and stand crying in the stables. The blind old dogs are starving to death because they're not used to the bad food. You're not allowed to buy meat or bones for the dogs at the store, and the porridge the aunts make for them gets secretly eaten up by that Donna as soon as the aunts turn their backs. Poor Musti has been dead a week now. When Aunt Louise ordered Donna to go out into the garden to dig a grave for him, she refused. Aunt Malla had to put the body on the veranda and cover it with a rug. The poor dead dog would have stayed there unburied today if Oliver hadn't taken a spade and crow-bar and gone out into that awful cold. But the very worst of all was when Sorkka and Palonen had come to search the house at Salmela.

I can still see Aunt Louise in front of me as she was telling us about it, hissing and spluttering like a kettle when it boils over – little drops of spit flying around and her mouldy eyes glowing dimly. Everything about her was shaking – her hands, her wrinkled cheeks, the woollen stocking dangling by her ear. She picked up a knife from the table and waved it about to threaten Sorkka. Aunt Malla sat with her hands in her lap, crumpling up her lace handkerchief and nodding in confirmation of everything Aunt Louise said. And Aunt Gulla turned round on the couch now and again with a heavy sigh so that it creaked and squeaked underneath her. Worst of all was that she was crying, her cheeks glistening with tears. I was ashamed to look in her direction because I didn't want her to notice I had seen it.

Sorkka and Palonen had come at the head of thirty Reds and made a terrible noise outside. The Crane had gone to meet them, bowed and asked them to go away. Every sensible person must realize that three old ladies have other things to do besides making bombs or hiding machine-guns in cupboards. But the Reds just laughed and chased Crane away with their bayonets. Then they broke open the front door and clumped in without either wiping their feet on the doormat or even taking off their caps. One of the ruffians tried to teach Popotjka rude words – Aunt Malla had been standing beside him and had to go to bed afterwards but didn't get a wink of sleep all night. Another ruffian took Aunt Gulla by the waist and tried to lift her out of her armchair – a wild bearded man with straw in his hair and huge fists, filthy with wagon grease and God knows what. He just laughed foolishly when Aunt Gulla was left there gasping, with dirty marks on her dress and cheeks and unable to say a word.

They poked their noses into everything, looking under beds, sticking their bayonets right through mattresses and bolsters and pulling dresses and fur boas out of the wardrobes. But they would never have found anything if that Donna hadn't told them about General Grund's sword and pistols Aunt Malla had hidden in the Turkish couch. Palonen confiscated the pistols and Sorkka took the sword with the mother-of-pearl sword-belt and gold braid. He fastened it round his waist and clumped down the front steps like a puffed-up rooster.

When the Reds came outside again, Crane considered enough was enough. She ran after Sorkka, screeching that he should give back the sword and its valuable belt immediately. At first Sorkka took no notice but continued on towards the carts waiting by the entrance. But when Crane jabbed at him with her beak, he grew angry, turned round and gave her a terrible kick. She started running away through the snow, her neck stretched out and wings outspread, shrieking for help. Perhaps some wing-feathers had snapped or one wing was broken, but she was unable to take off and fly away. Sorkka followed her and tried to kick her again, but then he slipped and fell backwards. The ruffians all howled with laughter, but Sorkka was simply enraged. He swore loudly, spat on his hand and pulled the sword out of its sheath. Crane had almost reached the door the aunts were holding open when Sorkka caught up with her. He raised his arm and the sword flashed. Something small and grey soared away across the road and made a red hole in the snowdrift. Crane went on running and flapping without her head and then collapsed in a pool of blood in front of the aunts on the steps.

We are already far out on the lake, the wind pricking my face with a thousand tiny pins. It's horrid thinking about the cold black water under the runners and all the frozen stiff monsters imprisoned down there looking at us through the ice. Sometimes it rolls and booms under us and echoes from shore to shore. Suddenly I catch sight of Sorkka, crouching down out there on the white expanse, enveloped in a black cloak. He's sitting quite still, waiting for us to come closer.

'Do you see?' I whisper, pointing at Sorkka. 'Shouldn't we turn round and go another way?'

'Oof,' says Bernt. 'You can't be afraid of everything. It might be a worker putting out nets in the ice-hole.'

At first, Sorkka is a little black dot in all that whiteness, but now he's growing and is outlined more and more clearly against the snowdrifts. He lowers his head and pulls his hood over his face so we can't recognize him.

'Stop!' I plead. 'Can't you see it's Sorkka?'

But Bernt goes on quite unconcerned. It's rumbling and booming underneath us again, startling me, and then I hear Sorkka tittering – softly so that you can hardly hear him.

But when we're quite close and it's already too late to turn round and escape and I'm just waiting for Sorkka to rush up, he suddenly dissolves and I don't recognize him any longer. He has turned into a juniper bush someone has stuck into the snow and behind the juniper bush there's a black hole in the snow, the edges iced up and full of sharp icicles, so that it looks like the wide-open mouth of a huge fish. Sorkka has made that hole in the ice to push everyone into when they come too close to the edge. We don't go near the edge because we know how dangerous it is, but stand at a distance looking down into the silent black water.

When we go on and I turn round, the juniper bush has gone and Sorkka is crouching down there again on the ice. He's terribly angry that he didn't succeed in tempting us. I can see him grinding his teeth and raising his blood-stained hands to the sky. But Bernt kicks off and jabs the spike even harder into the ice. The sledge flies along so that all I can see below me when I look down are white streaks. The singing behind us has stopped now – it whistles, howls, booms and rumbles, the shores clashing, and I can feel the whole covering of ice quaking with anguish. Sorkka must be quite near now. I can hear him panting and grinding his teeth. But Bernt is faster than he is. The next moment, we are rushing between swaying brown reeds, the kick-sledge takes a little hop and stops on the shore. When I turn round, Sorkka has flown back and is sitting far out on the ice as before. He is a black dot in all that white.

But the danger isn't over yet. As we approach the dairy, Bernt tells me to say nothing. Riika is standing in the middle of the road, a rifle over her shoulder, the bayonet fixed. The sack I'm sitting on suddenly feels unpleasantly hard. My heart is thumping and my knees are shaking. What shall I do if Riika orders me to get up and pokes at me with her bayonet? I can already see that she knows everything. Although she keeps one eye shut as always so as not to show that blood-red hole under the eyelid, the other eye stares straight through me, straight at the sack, and she knows all right that it's not a cushion.

We are quite quiet as we go past her and greet her. Behind me I can hear Bernt panting quickly. I'm already prepared to jump down from the sledge before Riika asks us anything at all. But to my surprise Riika's crooked face brightens into a friendly smile. She nods to us and calls: 'Hullo, boys. Get off home, quick now, and get warm!'

GRANDMOTHER IS READING:

'God is jealous, and the Lord revengeth; the Lord revengeth, and is furious; the Lord will take vengeance on his adversaries, and he reserveth wrath for his enemies!'

She turns the page of the Bible:

'The mountains quake at him, and the hills melt, and the earth is burned at his presence, yea, the world, and all that dwell therein. Who can stand before his indignation? and who can abide in the fierceness of his anger? his fury is poured out like fire, and the rocks are thrown down by him.'

It's boring just sitting still and listening. Grandmother goes on and on reading and just won't stop. You can understand why God is absolutely furious at this moment, but all the same I think Grandmother doesn't have to quarrel and threaten so terribly. When all is said and done, the fact that everything on earth is upside-down is not our fault but Sorkka's and Palonen's. Why do we have to sit here listening to Grandmother calling for God's vengeance on the Reds? She might just as well talk to God on her own, the two of them together. If she goes on provoking him like this, he might get so angry he'll destroy the whole world and wipe out the innocent as well as the guilty, because when you're really angry you don't have time to think about what you're doing. You smash everything you can lay your hands on and don't regret things until afterwards when you see you've destroyed things you like.

'Riki,' says Grandmother. 'Sit still and stop playing about.'

I jump and let go the armchair tassels in fright.

'Woe to the bloody city! it is all full of lies and robbery; the prey departeth not.'

I look at my hands folded on my lap. They itch rather, the skin over the knuckles shiny and peeling, though the swelling has gone and the hole grown over. I always want to scratch those places with my nails and poke away the bits of skin, although Aunt says I mustn't do that. I glance at her and start picking off the round scab on my forefinger. It feels good although it hurts a little.

'Riki,' whispers Aunt, leaning forward. 'Fold your hands and sit up straight.'

Grandmother looks at us over her glasses for a moment and when it's quiet again, she lowers her head and goes on:

'The noise of a whip, and the noise of the rattling of the wheels, and of the prancing horses, and of the jumping chariots.

'The horseman lifteth up both the bright sword and the glittering spear: and there is a multitude of slain, and a great number of carcases; and there is none end of their corpses; they stumble upon their corpses.'

Suddenly shouts and noises penetrate through the window. They must be just outside the house. The voices are angry and menacing, but there's nothing to be seen out there. The trees cast long blue shadows and the snow crust sparkles so that it hurts your eyes. Mamma exchanges a look with Aunt and shifts uneasily in her chair. Aunt makes a little move as if to get up, but both stay where they are when Grandmother goes on reading. The noise outside just gets worse, so in the end Grandmother closes the Bible and says: 'Well, what is it this time? I really must say . . .'

'Something must have happened,' says Mamma, giving Grandmother a blank frightened look.

We jump down and rush over to the kitchen. A whole crowd of people are shouting and yelling on the road in front of the house, including Hämäläinen and Ali, Riika and Kuri Mari, as well as a bunch of workers' children running around in and out between their boots and skirts. Two men in black overcoats come staggering through the snow. They're walking crookedly, their hands behind their backs and their collars turned up. Both are covered from head to foot with snow, and one of them has lost his hat. Behind them is old Katri the washerwoman with her rifle in her hand, urging them on with the bayonet.

'They're spies,' says Njanja, from by the kitchen window. 'They've been caught on the Viborg road when they were trying to mine it.'

They are all yelling and waving their hands about out there as they surround the two nasty wicked spies. Then the whole crowd starts moving towards the barn. Aunt presses her face against the window-pane and sighs.

'Dear Lord! Now they're going to shoot them.'

'Get away from the window, children!' shrieks Mamma. 'You might be killed if you're not careful.'

I curl up in the corner between the kitchen table and the wood box and hold my breath so that Katri won't find out where I've hidden. Then Grandmother also comes into the kitchen and goes over to the window. 'How odd,' she says, shading her eyes with her hand. 'It's Metzler and Sus!'

Mamma and Aunt rush out, leaving the porch door open. It's cold and I think: now Katri will take Mamma and Aunt to the barn, too, and put them in that red hollow where little Jonah was killed, then they'll shoot them.

There's a terrible racket going on outside, worse than when the chickens, turkeys and geese collect round the muck-heap and all squawk at once. Then suddenly it is quiet. And they all laugh.

After a while Mamma and Aunt come back with the two uncles. They shake themselves like dogs when they come in, brushing off the snow so that it spatters all over the walls and melts in big silvery patches on the carpet. One uncle is swearing about his galosh which got stuck in a snowdrift, and he stamps so hard on the floor, I run away.

When they've finally brushed themselves down in the living-room, I see they're not Uncle Metzler and Uncle Sus at all, but two perfect strangers. For Uncle Sus is usually stern and dignified, has his shiny pince-nez fixed to his nose and a great wavy mane of hair. By no means has he got a bloated red face framed by wet curls or small peering eyes that see nothing. And he usually lifts Tommy up and calls him Riki.

And Uncle Metzler had a young handsome face and didn't look like an old pirate with a black beard covering his lips and coming right down his chest. This uncle reminds me of that cruel Kuna Grim and looks so dangerous I daren't go over to greet him. I can't understand why Grandmother should be so completely mistaken as to call one of them 'Sus dear' and allow the other one to kiss her hand. Katri and the others out there were probably right to suspect there was something fishy about the uncles, so took them prisoner. Perhaps they really are spies and very dangerous and wicked, and perhaps it would have been better if they'd been shot over by the barn.

As we're sitting round the table drinking real tea from St Petersburg, the false uncles tell us that they were walking along the Viborg road and came across Katri the washerwoman at the crossroads where the Lavola road turns off. She held up her rifle like a barrier across the road and shouted: 'Halt! Password!'

The uncles took no notice of her and just walked on, so Katri threatened them with her bayonet, but one of the uncles brushed the gun aside and they started running. Katri yelled again: 'Halt! Halt!'

Then she fired and they ran even faster. She shot the hat off the false Uncle Metzler's head, and she would have shot off his actual head if the uncles hadn't jumped down into a ditch and taken cover. But the snowdrifts were terribly deep and the uncles sank down in the snow right up to their eyes and couldn't get out again. Katri came rushing up with her rifle, ordered them to crawl out of the drifts, then tied their hands behind their backs. They weren't even allowed to look for the pince-nez or the galosh they had lost in the snow. Katri just shooed them ahead with her bayonet.

THE WAR IS ALREADY SO CLOSE YOU CAN HEAR IT
rumbling beyond the forest, though there's still nothing
to be seen. When you walk along the Viborg road, you can
hear bangs on the other side of the lake and shots rattling
in the forest behind us, just as if someone had fired back
from there. Far away behind King's Mountain it rumbles
and booms like a thunderstorm. You can feel the sound
come rolling under the ground, bumping into barns, hills
and forest, making them jump, then exploding into a
short dry bang. King's Mountain's bare, snow-covered
ridge is hidden in grey mist. Bernt says it's on fire over
there and it's the guns rumbling like that.

One day when Tommy and I were walking along the
Viborg road, with Njanja pushing Baby ahead of her in
a sledge, we started laughing every time there was a
bang or a crash. It was tremendous fun and exciting as
there was such a lot of firing. But Njanja told us not to
laugh. 'War's nothing to laugh about,' she said, crossing
herself when another crash came. 'Gospodi pomilui!
Don't forget my sinful soul! Hold your hand over us all
so that we are saved from damnation!'

But I refused to obey her and Tommy always did
whatever I did. We laughed even more, hopping about
and shouting as loudly as we could.

'Bang!'

'Crash!'

'Brmmmmmmmmboommmm!!'

'Huh, nasty horrible brats!' cried Njanja. 'People
shot, old people and mothers burnt alive, little children

starving to death, and all you do is laugh! I'll learn you!
Vot!'

She left Baby in the sledge, broke off some brushwood and came trotting towards us. I stuck out my
tongue and we ran away as fast as we could. Njanja
is so fat and heavy and finds it so hard to run, it's
not at all difficult to escape from her. But Tommy got
stuck in a snowdrift and was caught. I heard him yelling
behind me and saw Njanja holding him by the collar and
shaking him so that he kept choking and trying to catch
his breath. I had managed to save myself across a ditch
and was out on the snow crust. I knew it would break
under Njanja if she ventured on to it.

Baby's sledge had been left on the road a little way
away from Njanja. She was still holding tight on to
Tommy and beating his backside and legs with the
brushwood. I ran over to the sledge, grabbed the handle
and rushed off, shooting it ahead of me. Baby smiled
as soon as he saw me, his mouth one great wide line,
his cheeks as round as little apples under his green
crocheted cap, his whole face shining like a moon. He
had surely never had such a fast ride in his life. I smacked
with my tongue and he laughed, raising his hands in
his little green bag-mittens and banging the covers with
them. Then I also began to think it all such fun, and I
ran faster and faster, although I could hear Njanja
shouting for me to stop.

Then we came to the slope and I rushed down it.
Everything went so quickly I could see nothing but white
flashing in front of my eyes and the air was whistling
round my ears as in windy weather. I suddenly noticed
I couldn't steer the sledge. It leapt up, swerved and ran
up into the snowdrifts along the side of the road. Before I
was thrown down and had rolled round, I saw the sledge
lurch, stand on edge and tip over.

By the time I had scrambled up and wiped the snow
out of my eyes, I saw what I had done. The sledge was
upside-down, its runners in the air, pillows and covers

strewn around, and far away in among the snowdrifts on the other side of the ditch I could see the bundle that was Baby, screaming terribly. He had lost his cap and one mitten and his hair and clothes were covered with snow. He was wriggling like a worm, lifting up the shapeless bottom half of his body, which was stuffed inside a blue cloth bag. His face was one huge wide-open mouth and his whole body was shaking and tense as he bawled away. His screams were so terrible, he was clearly about to burst and die at any moment. I lifted him up, but then he started bawling even more loudly. He was heavy and uncomfortable to hold in my arms. I thought I'd better throw him away at once and run away, because nothing could come of Baby any longer now, he looked so horrible. But by then Njanja had caught up with us and snatched Baby out of my arms. 'Well, now!' she said. 'Are you satisfied? I'll be telling the old lady about this, I certainly shall, mark my words!'

Then she said nothing more, but started fussing over Baby, now wailing away in her arms. She blew the snowflakes off his eyelashes and drooled away as if she herself were a baby. Then she pressed him to her so that he disappeared completely under her head-cloth, now loosened and covering them both like a tent.

I stood beside them without even considering running away, waiting for Njanja to hit me. But she just went on consoling Baby, picking up the scattered garments and shaking the snow off them. When I helped her and handed her a mitten or a shawl, she took them without saying anything or even looking at me. Then, when everything had been put in order again and Baby had been tucked into the sledge, she took Tommy's hand and walked homewards without turning round, just as if she hadn't noticed I was with them.

On the way home Baby stopped crying and was absolutely quiet. When I looked at him, he was lying there with his eyes closed, pale and unmoving.

'Is he dead now?' I asked.

'Tsch!' hissed Njanja. 'He's asleep.' Then she turned to me and said: 'Just you wait till we get home! You deserves to be skinned alive for this.'

There was a rumble behind us again. The booming rolled over us, spread out over the sky and burst into a series of dull thumps over on the horizon. It sounded threatening and angry, as if a whole lot of gigantic bearded uncles had been quarrelling beyond the blue ring of forests and mountains which is the boundary of the world.

Njanja crossed herself and sighed. 'Gospodi pomilui! Save my poor sinful soul!'

TOMMY AND I HAD LAGGED BEHIND AND HAD reached only as far as the ice-cellar when the booming was suddenly answered by a bellowing and shrill shouts from the byre. When we looked round, we saw Anna running at full tilt down the road, no kerchief on her head, her hair flowing and her face red. 'Run!' she was shouting. 'Look out! He's after me!'

I took Tommy by the hand and raced off towards home. Although we ran as fast as we could, I didn't think it was fast enough. Tommy tried to twist his hand out of my grasp and squealed at me to slow down. He tripped and fell headlong in the slush among the horse droppings. I tugged at his hand to get him up, but his mitten came off and I went on running with the empty mitten in my hand, not stopping until I was on the kitchen veranda.

'You got no wits in your head at all?' puffed Njanja, stumping up the steps and tripping over Baby's shawls. 'First you tries to kill the little one and now you goes and leaves Tommy in the lurch!'

I wanted to rush back, although I knew it would be no use. But there was nothing dangerous to be seen. Anna came running over the garden path, dragging Tommy with her. She leant over the balcony railing and looked out, the sleeve of her coat torn and the whole of the front wet and dirty. A bright red drop was trembling on her cheek-bone. 'He knocked me down,' she told Njanja. 'But it weren't too bad. Riika got between and then he charged at her.'

She ran the back of her hand across her cheek and smeared the drop into a brick-coloured streak. 'Worse for Riika,' she went on. 'He'd've finished her off completely if I hadn't started screaming and making a hell of a row. Then he left her and went for me.'

She coughed, held her side and grimaced. 'He's heading this way,' she gasped, pointing at the ice-cellar. 'Look!'

Bull's black head appeared over on the crown of the hill. He was approaching at a playful trot, a long chain rattling along behind him in the sledge-tracks, its links winking. He stopped immediately opposite the veranda, raised his moist muzzle and bellowed.

Someone knocked on the kitchen window behind us. Mamma's blazing eyes and pursed lips were just visible behind the pane. She was making angry signs for us to come in.

Njanja gathered up the shawls and covers round the huge bundle that was Baby. 'Vot!' she said, glaring at me. 'You laughs at the War and skipped off just now. You wouldn't listen to me. But no more laughing or skipping off for you now. Retribution comes sooner than you think.'

Bull approached the gatepost and sniffed at it. He was in no hurry. Finally he lowered his head and rubbed his horn against it.

'This is just a game. Look, this is what I do with your gatepost, because it amuses me. I'll soon be doing the same to you, Riki.'

The gatepost creaked, snapped off and fell to the ground. The whole fence on the left heaved up with a screech of complaint, folded over and was left hanging flat over the drifts.

Njanja turned round with the bundle in her arms.

'I ought to lock the door and leave you out here, my goodness. So him over there could take care of you!'

But I was quicker than Njanja.

Through the kitchen window we could see him sauntering to and fro across the empty yard. He seemed vexed that we had run away and hidden from him. He was angrily lashing his tail and the chain was sliding through the snow like a glittering snake. Although all the doors and windows were barred, my teeth chattered every time he bellowed. It sounded like a trumpet-blast before an attack. Now he was approaching the kitchen veranda and disappeared behind the railings. Something rolled away with a dull rumble and thumped against the house. I could feel the kitchen table trembling underneath me and jumped down. The ceiling and the walls seemed to sway as if made of cardboard.

'Aunt,' I whispered, clutching at her skirt. 'Hold the door, Aunt. He's coming in. He's knocking the house down.'

'He can't knock it down,' said Aunt, putting her hand on my head so that I soon felt better. 'That was probably only the water-tub he knocked off the stand.'

'Boshe moi! Dear Lord! The water-tub!' grumbled Njanja, waddling up to the window. 'Where am I to get water from when I have to get the dinner? Vot! Tjort vosmij!' She thrust out her jaw and clenched her fist.

'Go away, damned great hulk, you, great horned Satan, you! I wants to go to the cellar for turnips and to the woodshed for wood. Get away with you!'

'He won't go,' said Anna. She was sitting with her stocking pulled down, her knee badly grazed, cleaning the sores with some cotton wool. 'I know him. He's as stubborn as sin.'

'Look, Marfa Nikolajevna!' cried Aunt. 'He's pulling the washing off the line and tossing it all over the place.'

Njanja threw the window open, her face scarlet, her cheeks trembling like jelly. 'Get away with you!' she screamed. 'Off! Out! Don't you hear me? What you want to come fooling around here for, you great nuisance you, bloodthirsty creature that you is!'

The Grown-ups were sitting squabbling round the tea-table in the living-room. No one had time to think about what I'd done to Baby or to punish me for it.

Mamma was complaining to Grandmother, her voice whining and accusing, as if everything was Grandmother's fault and owing to Grandmother's not wanting to intervene and put things right. Grandmother sat there saying nothing. She was very pale and her mouth was tight shut. The hand hanging over the arm of the chair was holding a holy book with black leather covers and gold edges, the tassel of a bookmarker sticking out of it. Uncle Metzler was sitting all hunched up, sipping his cooling tea, now and again frowning worriedly and glaring at Mamma, as if he had a guilty conscience. Uncle Sus was walking up and down with his chest thrown out and his head back, now and again running his hand over his wavy mane of hair. He was looking very dignified and grave. 'I know,' he said. 'An angry bull is nothing to play around with. One single incautious step, one single miscalculated swing of the hips, and you're dead.' He spun round on his heel and thrust his thumbs under his waistcoat so that it stuck out at the armholes. 'I saw that in Madrid. The matador miscalculated and the bull jabbed its horn into his belly. He hung on the bull's head and slowly heeled over like an insect impaled on a pin . . .'

'Can't we get a message to Uncle Georg?' Mamma broke in, looking appealingly round her. 'Perhaps he knows what we ought to do?'

Uncle Sus replied with an ambiguous Hmm! and went and stood with his back to us by the window, the snowy garden just visible beyond him. Bull's bouncing dark back glided past and was shattered in the glass like a jigsaw puzzle.

'He's still there, the rogue. No dinner for us at this rate.' He turned, adjusted his glasses and looked around with his nose in the air. 'We must do something about this. Up you get, Ernest! It's no good sitting twiddling your thumbs and just waiting.'

'What are you going to do?' asked Uncle Metzler, clearing his throat.

'Act! Do something! Fight! What the hell's the point of sitting here?'

'But isn't it a trifle unwise – without any kind of experience. You yourself said just now that a raging bull . . .'

'Experience!' Uncle Sus swept away all objections with an elegant gesture. 'A simple country bull, ignorant and untrained, which has never been in a bullring. He'll be frightened and run away as soon as he sees us, I assure you.'

'But shouldn't we anyhow have some kind of weapon?' the other uncle broke in, reluctantly rising to his feet, his shoulders hunched and back bowed as he looked inquiringly around.

'With or without weapons! What matter? In Lisbon, bullfighters fight with their bare hands. I saw six matadors standing in a line behind each other with their arms folded across their chests. The bull charged straight at the first one. He grasped it by the horns and the other matadors clung on to it. Before it could blink, the bull was beaten to his knees.'

'Yes, well, all that's very interesting,' growled Uncle Metzler impatiently. 'But you're no Portuguese bullfighter and neither are we in Lisbon at the moment. And when you last told that story, you said you'd never been to Lisbon. You said we ought to emigrate there – and now you've already been there.'

'Me – never been to Lisbon – what nonsense!' hissed Uncle Sus. 'Me!' He took off his glasses, then went and stood in front of Uncle Metzler and waved them about in front of the uncle's face.'Just tell me something, Ernest. You, sitting here, lying low so comfortably and safely. Have you the nerve to speak like that to me, whom you wish to leave in the lurch and force to fight with a raging bull? I must say I am surprised, to say the least – and if you don't change your tone soon, all is over between us, Ernest!'

He took a few steps back to show what a great distance had now come between him and Uncle Metzler, and raised his hand.

'But I never said I wouldn't come with you.' Uncle Metzler was also worked up now. 'On the contrary, I am not frightened. I just don't like that sort of damned talk. I think. . . .'

The uncles shouted at each other for a while but finally calmed down. Uncle Sus stalked out of the room with an offended expression on his face. Uncle Metzler went sighing after him, taking two ski sticks with him from the hall. We heard the front door slamming.

However much we looked out of the window, we could see nothing of Bull. But we saw the uncles creeping through the garden with long, slow strides, holding the ski sticks in front them like spears, Uncle Sus ahead. Every now and again he crouched down, peered around and raised a warning hand to Uncle Metzler. Suddenly Uncle Metzler leapt up and took cover behind the corner of the house. We could see him excitedly waving at Uncle Sus, but either Uncle Sus ignored him or he hadn't noticed. He was behind the garden bench with one knee thrust forward and the other leg stretched backwards. Slowly he raised the ski stick with the point directed in front of him.

Then Bull suddenly appeared in the garden from the opposite direction. He stopped right in front of the window, where a few dead flower stems were protruding out of a snow-covered flower-bed, and glowered thoughtfully at Uncle Sus's sloping back. Finally he let out a darkly mocking laugh. Uncle turned round and slowly straightened both legs. That went on for a terribly long time – as if he were balancing on a rope and was afraid of any violent unforeseen movement. The ski stick in his hand was shaking and the creases in his trousers were fluttering. Bull stood still and glowered. He seemed to have bewitched the uncle by the garden bench with his gaze. Without taking his eyes off the uncle, he slowly lowered his head and aimed his horns at the uncle's stomach. The uncle was as rigid as a tree.

Suddenly Uncle Sus let out a shrill yell, grabbed the ski stick with both hands and struck several times in the direction of Bull without hitting anything except the ground between them. Then he flung away the ski stick and rushed off, still yelling in a shrill unnatural voice. Bull started back at first, then hurled himself with a bellow at the garden bench, tipping it over and ripping off the lathes. Splinters of wood and bits of ice swirled around, a shattered plank sailed away like a shadow and landed with a clatter on the icy path in front of the veranda steps.

It already looked as if Bull had won when Uncle Metzler suddenly rushed out from behind the corner of the house, swung the ski stick above his head and struck Bull in the side with it. The blow was so hard, the uncle bounced up in the air like a rubber ball. Bull gave a little leap and turned towards him. They danced round in a swirl of snow and steam. The uncle kept on hitting, but the bamboo split on Bull's horns, the stick bent and the blows became a twittering birdlike sound. Then they were gone, the garden was deserted and all we could see was the grubbed-up snowdrifts, the shattered garden bench and Uncle Sus's discarded ski stick a little way away from it. Suddenly Uncle Sus came racing at full tilt along the garden path, then stopped so suddenly he lost his balance and almost fell over. He flung his arms up in the air and fled back at the same speed. Soon after, Uncle Metzler came running from the opposite direction, covered from head to foot in snow and as spotty as a leopard. Then Bull swept past in a storm of fragments of ice and snow, scattering them against the window-pane.

A moment or so later we heard the uncles clumping in through the kitchen entrance, arguing and swearing fearfully.

'Cowardly wretch, you!' hissed Uncle Metzler, furiously brushing off snow so that the wallpaper was covered with dark patches. 'It was all your fault. You kept well out of the way all the time I was fighting Bull.'

He couldn't find his muffler, which was hanging down his back, and he kept spinning round to get hold of it.

'But I've always known that. You're cowardly and unreliable . . .'

'Who?' shouted Uncle Sus, straightening up. 'Who is cowardly and unreliable? Who faced Bull alone? And who hid behind the corner of the house? I did happen to have the misfortune to drop my ski stick. I was forced to make a tactical retreat. But you. . . .' He thrust his hands into his pockets and looked Uncle Metzler up and down with a dignified gaze.

'Tactical retreat!' said Uncle Metzler scornfully. 'You ran away as if you'd peed in your pants . . .'

'Silence!' roared Uncle Sus.

They looked each other up and down, all ready to go for each other. Uncle Metzler clenched his fists and thrust out his lower jaw like a pike. They were so inflamed by their battle with Bull that they knew they had to find some excuse to fight all over again. But when Grandmother appeared in the doorway, they soon quietened down and went off, each in a different direction.

DUSK WAS FALLING. THE REFLECTION OF THE LAMP in the window-pane glowed like a furnace. Sometimes I thought I could make out Bull's dark body behind the reflection, but when I looked closer it was only branches of trees swaying back and forth. As soon as I closed my eyes, I could see him circling round the house and glaring hungrily in at the windows, his tongue hanging out and now and again licking his lips.

Grandmother looked round disapprovingly.

'Is Bull still there?'

'Yes,' said Aunt. She turned round, Baby on her arm, and absently stroked his head. 'He's broken down the door of the woodshed and pushed his way in there. But now he's somewhere out there again and God knows what he's up to.'

'I don't understand why he doesn't go away,' complained Mamma. 'It's as if they'd set him on us and left him here on purpose.'

'Strange,' said Aunt. 'He's come over us like a judgement.'

Grandmother looked searchingly from the one to the other then finally fixed a long look on me. She was staring so strangely, I could feel my cheeks glowing and turned my face away so that the others shouldn't notice.

Something flapped out there. The whole sky flared up and turned pink. Then it was all over. The booming rolled around in the darkness, thumping and banging

Grandmother looked up at the ceiling, closed her eyelids as if asleep, then said slowly: 'Anyone with a clear conscience and who follows God's word has no need to fear his punishment. Come, children,' she went on, sinking down into an armchair. 'Let us pray and invoke God so that he lets these afflictions turn away from us. Would you be so kind as to fetch my glasses, please, Anni.'

When Grandmother had been given her glasses, she went and sat at the piano and we stood in a semicircle round her. I didn't know whether I'd dare join in the singing with the others. The holy force pouring out from Grandmother seemed to reject me. But Aunt grasped my arm and pushed me into the circle so that I ended up standing just behind Grandmother's chair.

Grandmother's fingers slid indecisively over the keys a few times, then she put her hands on her lap, lowered her head and listened. Black horns were sticking out behind chairs and tables. Something was singing hollowly through its nose inside the tiled stove. There was a dreadful noise going on outside. The house was creaking and shuddering. Sometimes the window-panes tinkled, some kind of flying creature whirling round the house and bumping against the glass in passing to look in. Again and again the window flared up. Bull appeared like a black mountain, then hurtled rumbling back down into the darkness.

'Now let's begin,' said Grandmother, lifting her hands and bringing her curled outspread fingers down on to the keys. We sang:

'Our Lord to us a vast fortress is. . . .'

Aunt's singing was the strongest. She stood with her mouth open, frowning heavily, but Grandmother's high penetrating voice drowned even hers. Mamma and Bernt were also singing, and what with the bell-like tolling of the piano and the surging sound of the singing, the noise outside faded. I could feel the holy force pouring out from the singing and filling the house, turning it into a fortress with towers and pinnacles, deep moats outside.

The wrathful Prince of Darkness
Doth to the earth us trample;
Great powers and much cunning
His armour is assured;
No match has he on earth!

Although Bull out there rose like a mountain with
clouds clinging to his shoulders and the moon between
his horns, he didn't aspire to our fortress, which shot
higher and higher into the heights and finally plunged
its pinnacles through the canopy of the sky. Angels with
dazzling shields and raised swords took their places at
the apertures and up on the walls, and there, up above
the highest tower, God floated on a golden cloud in a
wreath of rays. Bull was circling down there round
the base of the fortress, bellowing with hunger and
disappointment, but his cry did not reach us. The
ringing of Grandmother's playing penetrated through
the apertures in the tower and welled out over the world
like a message of consolation and victory.

'Why aren't you singing?' whispered Aunt, leaning
over. 'Keep your hands clasped! Can't you see what the
others are doing?'

I clasped my hands, looked at Bernt and moved my
lips so that Aunt would think I was singing. Perhaps
Aunt thought I was not entirely one of the ungodly, as
she wanted me to sing together with the others. I could
feel the holy force pouring into me and filling me with a
pleasing numbness.

When Grandmother stopped singing, there was silence outside the window. The wind had dropped and
the rumbling over from the forest had stopped, the stars
shining above the tree-tops like glittering little dots. It
had grown lighter. The lamp was shining cosily and the
reflection in the window-pane was now like a great open
tiger-lily. The horrid horns had gone. You could see now
that they were quite ordinary shadows of the knobs on the

chair arms and the tiled stove's damper thrown on to the wall.

We heard the screech of the kitchen door and Njanja clumped in with her arms full of wood. She flung the logs down in front of the stove, wiped her hands on her apron and breathed out. 'Him's gone,' she said. 'The damned critter.' She spat on her hand and crossed herself. 'I'm off down to the well for water now, and to the cellar for turnips.'

Everyone was surprised, only Grandmother sitting there saying nothing, her mouth pursed and a scoffing little smile on her lips.

'Katri took him back to the byre,' Njanja went on, brushing splinters and pieces of bark off her chest. 'He went with her as meekly as a lamb. I suppose he'd got cold hanging about here and was hungry – longing to go back to the byre.'

'Oh, just think, Katri,' sighed Aunt. 'Who'd have believed she was so brave?'

'She's the worst of the lot of them,' said Mamma. 'A real Red. Always swaggering about like a man with that rifle and those boots.'

While we were having dinner the sound of sleigh-bells came from the road and a sledge stopped outside the front door. Someone banged on the kitchen door and we could hear a mumble of voices. The kitchen door screeched again and again as heavy footsteps clumped up the steps.

After a while Njanja appeared in the doorway and said to Grandmother: 'They're here with him and want you to tell them what to do.'

Grandmother hurriedly wiped her mouth on her table-napkin and rose to her feet. Njanja wanted to explain something, but at that moment some dark figures pushed their way into the room. One of them was walking backwards carrying something that wouldn't go through the door and bumped against the doorpost.

'Hold the door open,' yelled someone. 'That's it. Now we can . . .'

'Wouldn't it be better in the kitchen?' Mamma stammered, looking at Grandmother. 'Why do they have to. . . .'

But Grandmother shook her head. 'It's lighter here and there's more space.' She nodded towards the intruders. 'That's all right. Put him down now, but carefully.'

The man walking backwards bumped into me with the worn shiny seat of his pants, so I almost fell over and I hit my arm against the arm of a chair. When I had moved aside so as not to be trampled on by everyone crowding round me, I recognized Hämäläinen and Pekka slowly crouching down and placing a stretcher on the floor.

'Slowly, slowly, for God's sake,' cried someone. 'Don't tip the stretcher.'

I could just catch a glimpse of a black cloth spread over someone lying on the stretcher, but then there were so many people in the way, I couldn't see anything properly.

I heard someone crying behind me. Over by the stove I saw Kuri Mari pressing her apron to her mouth and whimpering as if she had toothache. Some farm girls in red woolly caps and striped stockings slipped silently in through the door and pressed themselves against the wall, their heads sullenly bowed, now and again rubbing their eyes with their knuckles.

'The sheets must be in the bottom drawer on the left.' Grandmother cleared her throat and looked round the room with a disapproving expression. 'There's such a crush in here, one can hardly move,' she said. 'Ask them to wait in the kitchen. And send the children out. They're only in the way here.'

But it took awhile before anyone got hold of me and pushed me into the nursery. I managed to wriggle my way up to the stretcher and saw an upturned face between Uncle Sus's and Hämäläinen's legs. The head was bandaged with a blood-stained cloth that covered the cheek and one eye. The other eye was closed and he was snoring as if asleep. A red bubble ballooned out of his lips, burst with a pop, then started growing again.

Afterwards we saw a lantern bobbing away in the darkness from the kitchen window. It looked like a lost star wandering about out there, searching for something. Streaks of snow and branches appeared, then plunged again into darkness, the gatepost's shadow grew longer and longer, then swung round like the hand of a watch. Finally the light stopped and flared. The darkness cracked open – a bit of the road, a sledge with a horse harnessed to it and high up in the dark the swaying branches of the pines. The driver and the horse were black and threw a gigantic shadow diagonally across the drifts right up to our window. We saw the driver bend down, pick up his whip and rap the horse across the back. The sleigh-bells began jingling. The star slid quickly away and I could see nothing but the reflection of the lamp and my own face in the window-pane.

'Aunt, what did Bull do to him? Why was he snoring so peculiarly?'

'It wasn't Bull,' sighed Aunt. 'It was the War.'

THE NEXT MORNING EVERYTHING WAS UPSIDE-DOWN.
A great deal happened while we were out for our usual
walk before breakfast. The Reds were there again.

Two sledges were standing outside our front door,
their shafts decorated with red ribbons. A number of
peculiar figures in black and brown leather coats and
rifles with fixed bayonets were crowding round the
sledges. A soldier with a bandaged arm was standing
on the kitchen balcony, drinking water from the tub
out of our scoop. We made a wide detour through the
garden and crept into the house. Aunt pushed us into
the nursery without even taking off our outdoor clothes
and closed the door from the outside. No one took any
notice of us.

Bernt stood over by the window looking out over the
empty white meadow towards the forest. 'They're here
looking for Uncle Sus and Uncle Metzler,' he said. 'The
uncles have hidden in the forest.'

'How do you know that?'

'Quiet!' said Bernt. 'You mustn't talk so loudly.
They might hear. . . .'

I looked at the forest as sharply as I could to see if the
uncles' faces were looking out anywhere, but the forest
was just one great big, silent dark blue wall. They had
hidden themselves so well you couldn't see them.

They had skied past here early that morning. It had
been terribly windy, all the trees swaying and waving
their branches threateningly as if to stop them, their
overcoats blowing up and billowing out at the back,

177

as though someone were holding the hem and dragging them backwards. They couldn't make any headway, although they struggled and struggled with all their might. Uncle Metzler held on to his hat and kept losing one ski, then limping back and forth in the snow. Uncle Sus's legs kept sliding apart so you thought he would split in two. In the end he was blown right over and couldn't get up again for a long while. Over and over again he got his skis, sticks and legs so entangled he kept falling on his backside. Aunt and Njanja stood in the window laughing at them and saying the uncles would never get away. After a while they did indeed come back, their skis on their backs, both of them covered with snow and with ice in their hair and eyebrows. They maintained they'd seen Reds on guard over by the Lavola road and so they'd turned back.

'But why have they hidden in the forest?' I asked. 'Do they like that?'

'Because they're afraid and don't want to go to the War,' said Bernt. 'Maybe we'll have to go and hide in the forest, too. I heard Mamma say to Aunt that she would pack food and blankets. They might shoot us all and set fire to the house so that we all burn up.'

'But I don't want to go out into the forest. It's cold and dangerous, and the wolves might eat us up.'

'Silly, it'll be really nice sleeping in the forest. I'll build a wigwam and light a camp-fire. I've already dug out my bow and arrow, my penknife and my torch battery. You'd better get everything you need to take with you. But don't say anything to Tommy, because it's a secret. Mamma told Aunt not to tell us.'

'I'll take my sword and shield with me,' I said, for now I was really keen to be off. 'Can I come with you when you go hunting? Tell me. Can I?'

'Maybe.' Bernt's smile was teasing and rather superior. 'If you learn to walk quietly and promise to do everything I tell you.'

Then the door was suddenly jerked open and in came a tremendously tall man in a grey army cloak with a red band round his arm. He was so tall, at first I could see only the hem of his billowing cloak and his boots, which were pleated like an accordion and had jangling spurs at the back. The floorboards bounced as he put his heel down and all the things in the room started shaking and tinkling with fright. Mamma came in behind him, and she also looked very pale and frightened. Behind her I could just see Aunt's and Njanja's faces in the doorway.

The stranger spun round, looked about and growled. Then he strode over to the big wardrobe. Mamma hurried to open it for him. He nodded, looked hastily round the room again and went over to the door. On the threshold he stumbled and stepped on Jacko, whom I'd forgotten to hide away. He bent down and picked up the monkey and looked at it. Jacko looked very scared and appealingly raised both paws up above his head. I was also terrified, because I thought I'd never see him again. But the stranger didn't put Jacko in his pocket as I'd thought he would, but leant over me with the monkey in his hand. I was still so afraid, I didn't dare take Jacko from him. So he put him into my hand himself, patted my cheek and went out.

He smelt acrid and sharp like a wild animal. That smell reminded me a little of paraffin, a little of tobacco, a little of horse and a little of dog, and yet it wasn't any of those things, but something else, dangerous and unknown, something I couldn't make out. A powerful chill emanated from him, as if I'd been standing by an open window. The hand that touched me was cold and rough, and for a long while afterwards my cheek was numb, as if it wasn't mine at all.

'That was Sorkka!' said Bernt when we were alone again.

Then I was even more frightened when I thought about the hand that had patted me. I had to run to the mirror to make sure there wasn't a patch of blood on that cheek, but there was nothing there.

When we were allowed out of the nursery, Aunt was going round tidying up and Mamma was following her from room to room, talking about Sorkka and Palonen. 'Thank goodness,' she sighed. 'They didn't find the sacks of flour and oats I'd sewn into the bolster.'

She was crying. A strand of hair had come loose and was hanging down her face. I couldn't understand why she was crying and was so afraid. She ought to have been pleased Sorkka had been deceived and hadn't found anything.

Now it's booming and banging all over the place around the forest and mountains, so the windows rattle and the water swishes about in the carafe on Aunt's bedside table. Mamma and Aunt keep crying and it's awful to see. They behave like small children and aren't at all ashamed of themselves. You just can't understand how they could suddenly have become pitiful, scared and weak. Sometimes you think they're just pretending and trying to deceive you into being scared yourself.

In the evening the rooms are dark and horrible. Only one candle stump lit in the living-room, casting gigantic fluttering shadows up on the ceiling. Outside, the darkness is getting denser, neither the moon nor the stars visible, because they've all fallen out of the sky, but above the forest the sky is glowing with a hazy blood-red light. It spreads out, rising upwards to the bottom of the sky, and its rosy red glow is reflected in the snowdrifts. The whole earth, all the towns, forests and mountains are burning over there and the sky itself is beginning to catch fire. Cries and shouts can be heard from the road, as well as the hoofs of trotting horses. Then all is quiet again, but the red glow in the sky grows and shrinks, just like when you turn the lamp wick up and down.

Suddenly there's a terrible noise over in the darkness on the other side of the road. Blue flashes of lightning flare up and gunshots crack drily and abruptly, as when there's a clap of thunder quite close by. The soft velvety darkness splits apart over there and huge cornflower-blue flames flare up and go out, and in their glow occasionally dark contours of outhouses and black columns of pine trees appear like ghosts. It is so beautiful and so awful, I just stand staring at the window, although the shots are so loud I have to blink.

Suddenly Aunt comes rushing in and snatches me away from the window. She is terribly cross with me and takes me into Grandmother's room, where I have to sit on the floor pressed close to the stove and Mamma shouts at me every time I lift my head or try to straighten my legs out when they've gone numb under me.

At night I am woken up by a terrible bang. It's such a colossal bang, the ground shakes for a long time afterwards. It's pitch-dark and I don't know where I am, but something really terrible must have happened. The house must have been overturned and everything smashed to pieces – yes, perhaps the whole world has cracked open from top to bottom, as the bang was so great. Only gradually do I begin to make out other noises, dragging footsteps, the tinkle of glass, a voice whimpering and crying somewhere far away. I suddenly realize it's Tommy wailing. Then I give way to the fear and start bawling as loud as Tommy.

After a while Aunt is there with a candle in her hand. The room has come back and I see the house hasn't been overturned at all. Everything is in place and nothing is broken.

'Go to sleep, children,' says Aunt. She presses me back on to the pillow and tucks the covers round me. 'Go to sleep now. It was nothing to worry about.'

WHEN WE WAKE UP IN THE MORNING, THE SUNLIGHT
is lying in the wide trembling veins on the rag-rug, grains
of dust dancing and flickering above the window-sill, the
sky clear and blue outside. It's spring and the snowdrifts
are melting as fast as they can, rows of dark drops hanging
along the cornices of the roof. They free themselves, then
grow again. It is very quiet. All you can hear is the soft
thump of the drops off the roof and the twitter of a bird
outside. The world seems new and clean and everything
has a happy friendly look. Everything is in one piece and
in place.

The Grown-ups say the War is over. God and Kaiser
Wilhelm have been victorious over Sorkka and Palonen.
All the Reds have been taken prisoner and are awaiting
judgement. The Germans and the Whites have taken
Viborg and liberated us. We no longer need be afraid or
go into the forest to live among the wolves and monsters.
It's the workers' turn to be afraid now, because they were
friendly with the Reds. Simo, Hämäläinen, Pekka and
Katri have already run away and are hiding in the forest
on the other side of the meadow, just as the uncles did
awhile ago.

That terrible bang last night was caused by the
gunpowder store in Viborg exploding. Sorkka and Palonen set fire to it when they realized that they couldn't
escape and the hour of retribution had struck. They
wanted to blow the whole world to bits, but their devilish
plan failed. The world held, though the bang was so
awful the mirror in the living-room fell down and the

window in Grandmother's room cracked. Even in Viborg, only a few houses fell over and only Reds were killed by the explosion. It was a whole mountain of gunpowder they set fire to, and the bang was so great that not even Grandmother had ever experienced anything like it before.

The Reds had also meant to open the sluice-gates in Saima Canal to cause another Deluge. The water was to have rushed down over Viborg like Niagara Falls, then spread all over the world and drowned everything in its path, houses, forests and mountains, until not a single bare patch was left to stand on. Goodness knows what would have happened to us, as well as all the animals, for Grandmother hadn't been far-sighted enough to build an ark, and all the rowing-boats are still upside-down in the snowdrifts on the shore. At the last minute, just when Palonen had put his hand on the wheel that opens those horrible black sluice-gates, the Whites got to Juustila and the world was saved from the Deluge.

'Come and look, children,' says Aunt, taking us into the kitchen. 'The Whites'll soon be here.'

She lifts Tommy up on to the kitchen table in front of the window and tells me to get up on a chair and kneel there to look out. She's smiling in such a friendly way today, and talking and laughing so much, I'm no longer afraid of her. Njanja, too, has quite a new face, smiling out from under her grey woollen kerchief like a great friendly full moon. She says nothing about Tommy sitting on the table with his boots on or when I ruck up the rag-rug as I push the chair up to the window. She picks Baby from his basket and stands with him in her arms behind the table, looking through the window.

At first I can see nothing out of the ordinary, only the road and the trees beyond it. The road is covered with dirty grey mud, the melting snow filling the wheel-tracks and dark patches of horse droppings appearing between them. The road is empty and, although we wait for a long time, nothing comes along. The spruces wave their branches and a stalk sticking out of the snowdrift by the road is trembling with excitement.

Then we hear a heavy squelching that comes closer very quickly. A horseman gallops past and disappears down the slope by the ice-cellar. We just have time to see the mud splashing up from the horse's hoofs and the rider bouncing up and down as if he were on a rocking-chair. Both Tommy and I burst out laughing, because it was fun seeing him riding so quickly and the mud splashing up so high. But before we have time to stop laughing, a bunch of four more riders come past. They aren't riding so fast and you can see they've each got a white armband on. They are wearing long grey soldier's cloaks that cover the sides of the horses and have rifles on their backs. The riders bounce up and down, squelching and jingling, things hanging everywhere on straps, and strange things shaking up and down. Then more riders come all the time, one by one, or in larger groups. They're all wearing the same kind of grey cloaks and some have high white fur caps on their heads, but the horses are all different colours. Some are reddish-brown all over, some dark brown with light manes, some dappled greys and one is shiny black as if he'd been polished with shoe-cream. Actually, it's more fun looking at the horses than at the Whites. They glare so that the whites of their eyes show and a pink colour shines from their mouths and nostrils when they snort and bite on their bits.

Then no more riders come, and we think it's all over. But then a whole lot of of soldiers appear round the corner, marching in a double column, rifles on their shoulders and behind them horse-drawn wagons, then more soldiers and wagons. Suddenly the whole road as far as you can see is full of marching soldiers, snorting horses and lurching vehicles. Boots squelch in the mud, runners screech and wagon wheels splash through the puddles, sending up sprays of mud. We just stay watching, because we've never seen so many people, horses and loads all at the same time. No one can count them. There must be thousands – perhaps millions – of Whites going past. Some of them turn and wave to us when we call out and wave our hands behind the window-pane. Some of the vehicles swaying past look so funny that we can't help crying out in amazement and pointing at them. Whole small houses with canvas walls and canvas roofs come by and they lurch and sway so terribly you're afraid all the time they'll collapse and fall apart completely. Peculiar wagons like small engines rattle past on huge wheels, smoke pouring out of their chimneys and leaving little firebrands behind them in the slush. Then a team of three pairs of horses in a row come by, heaving and hauling as hard as they can, behind them lurching something huge and shapeless covered with a grey tarpaulin. The men running alongside it are shouting and yelling, slapping the reins and pulling at the horses' bits, and the horses dig their hoofs into the ground and jerk at the harness so that their knees and hindquarters tremble. Not until the amazing covered thing has rolled by do we see the mouth of the barrel of a huge gun sticking out of the canvas at the back. It is swaying slowly up and down and turns its empty black mouth towards us before disappearing behind the ice-cellar slope.

We also see a soldier leaving the road and standing in among the trees with his back to us, peeing a great yellow hole in the snow and taking no notice of Aunt and Njanja standing in the window watching. Two soldiers come up to the kitchen veranda, take the water-bucket and set off to the well to water their horses. Aunt and Njanja go out and talk to them by the entrance. They're happy and laugh all the time, and the soldiers are happy, too, smiling so that their teeth shine in their mouths. The horse stands with its nose in the bucket, drinking silently, sometimes snorting, lifting its head and letting the water run down out of the corners of its mouth. Njanja goes up to it and pats its shoulder and the horse twitches its ears and waves its tail to show that it's happy too, like everyone else that day.

Behind them, the road is still seething with soldiers, horses and vehicles. They pour along in an endless stream so that your eyes get tired from looking and you already wish it was all over, because you can't tell the difference any longer between what you are seeing at that moment and what you saw a moment ago. It is all endless tramping legs, squelching hoofs, white armbands and winking rifle barrels. And there's no difference whether you keep your eyes open or closed.

SMOKE IS POURING OUT OF THE BIG HOUSE chimney. At the front steps is a sleigh and inside it two shapeless bundles of clothing, a nose and a pair of eyes protruding from each one of them. They are Shura and Vova. When I get closer, Shura smiles uncertainly and calls out 'Hullo!', but Vova looks at me as if he didn't recognize me at all. His face is pale and transparent and his lower lip is trembling. Aunt Else comes down the steps and embraces him. She looks sad and her mouth is pursed as if she had a pin in it. She pretends not to see me, and orders Shura to come with her and carry Vova into the Big House. When Shura throws aside the rugs and shawls and gets out of the sleigh, he looks like a scarecrow. His jacket-tails reach down to his heels, the sleeves brush the ground and his trousers are pleated like an accordion. He must be wearing one of the uncles' suits. He flushes when our eyes meet and I refrain from asking why he is dressed so peculiarly, although I'd very much like to know. For a moment we stand looking at each other, because it's strange and unfamiliar to meet after such a long while. Finally I ask if he and Vova are to stay long at Teerilä.

'Yes,' says Shura. 'Grandfather says we have to live here now. Our whole house has burnt down.'

I want him to tell me more, but he doesn't have time, because Uncle Frans appears on the balcony and calls out to Shura to hurry up. Shura gives me a frightened look and shambles away like a bear cub, stumbling and putting out his hands for support, for his trousers have fallen down over his boots and are dragging in the slush.

As we go on, I see smoke is also pouring out of Uncle Erni's chimney. The curtains are drawn back and Aunt Mausi is standing on the kitchen steps beating the doormat. Uncle Volodja comes towards us from the barn in his peaked cap and ragged woollen jersey. He snatches off his cap, makes an elegant sweep with his arm and bows deeply. Then he asks if we like oranges. When Tommy says yes, he bends down and pinches Tommy's face in his hand so that his nose is almost pressed together between his cheeks, and Tommy becomes like a terrified little pig. 'There's the orange for you!' he says, laughing.

We go on. A flock of crows fly up from the tree-tops in front of us and soar off with hoarse cries towards the fields, and a black triangular sail rises over the snowdrifts that still cover large parts of the stubble fields. It can't be anyone else but Uncle Heinz taking a walk over there.

I am not told until we get home why all the uncles and aunts are back here at Teerilä again, and what happened when their house in Viborg was burnt down.

The Whites had penetrated right up to the outskirts of the town and had sent a scout up to the uncles' house, which was high up on the top of Papula Hill, and from the tower windows you could look down on the whole town as on a tray. But the Reds spotted the scout on the tower and started shooting at the house.

Everyone living there had to run down into the cellar to seek shelter when the grenades started crashing round the house and the windows shattered to pieces. Only Uncle Heinz refused to go anywhere. He pulled out his pocket-watch and said that the time for his midday nap had come. It was no use everyone beseeching him to go down with them. He let out a dreadful oath, waved his knobbly stick and limped off to his room. After a while the house got a direct hit. The uncles and aunts had to rush out into the snow in whatever they stood up in. One end of the house was already on fire and they had time to rescue only the barest necessities. Someone remembered Uncle Heinz and found him peacefully snoring in his bed. He was annoyed when they woke him and he refused to leave his room until he had dressed and packed a case. He was particularly upset that one of his sock suspenders had disappeared. The house was already a mass of flames when he finally made his way out, his face blackened, his eyebrows singed and a large burn-blister on his hand. The whole house burnt to the ground with tables and chairs, beds and clothes, books and toys and everything else in it.

I can see it all in front of me. Papula Hill, with that icy dizzy precipice I once passed when I was going to Viborg with Mamma – and the uncles' turreted villa clinging to the precipice. I can see the White scout leaning out of one of the turret openings with binoculars in his hand and the smoke-covered burning town below, where the guns of the Reds are rumbling and booming. I can see Sorkka and Palonen rushing up, turning the gun barrels and aiming, the grenades racing off like comets, flaring up on the top of the hill and going out. I can see the cellar where the uncles and aunts have fallen to their knees with clasped hands, tightly packed together like frightened mice, and Uncle Heinz peacefully stretched out in bed, while everything is banging and crashing round the house, blue flames flaring up outside and the curtain flapping at the shattered window. Suddenly there's a crash, beams splinter, broken-off table legs, arms of chairs, picture frames and pieces of porcelain fly around, but even then Uncle Heinz doesn't wake up. He's still snoring with his head on the pillow, although the room is full of dancing flames and the walls are red-hot, as if he were one of the three men in the burning fiery furnace Grandmother has told us about. Outside you can see the aunts and uncles running about like small grey shadows in the flickering light of the fire. They are counting their bundles, calling for help and weeping so that the tears pour down their cheeks. But Uncle Heinz is still inside. He buttons his braces, looks for his sock suspender under the bed, swearing and cursing. Everyone thinks he has long since been burnt up when the fire suddenly parts like a curtain and he comes out with his hair on fire like a torch and small flames dancing in his eyebrows.

Then they all rush down the hill with their bundles on their heads like Lot and his daughters as they fled from fiery Sodom, behind them the top of Papula Hill burning like a huge midsummer bonfire. You can see the flames flaring out of windows and the roof of the house. The whole building slowly collapses, sinking and disappearing in a column of fire, the sky full of swirling sparks, which fall slowly down on the path ahead of the feet of the fleeing people and go out with a hiss in the snow. But Uncle Heinz is still standing on a ledge with his case in his hand, looking up at the top of the hill. His one stocking has slid down and his underpants shine out from under his trouser-leg. 'My sock suspender! De De!' he is roaring, raising his stick to the skies. 'Sock suspender. De De. Damn and blast it!'

He is outlined against the flaming sky like a statue in black stone.

BERNT AND I WERE OUT HUNTING BIRDS TO TRY OUT HIS new catapult. Suddenly a horrible roar echoed behind the clump of trees that hide the stable buildings. We stopped and listened with some dismay, but fortunately it was fairly far away and didn't seem to be coming any closer. Bernt's face was pale and serious as he looked at me, and I had a horrid tickling feeling in my stomach.

'Must be Bull,' said Bernt. 'I wonder why he's bellowing like that. Something must have happened.'

We listened. Never before had his voice had such a fearful ring to it – not even when he was so angry over my getting the bilberry flan. The unfamiliar clang in his voice frightened me most of all because it meant you were uncertain whether it was even his. It sounded duller and darker, as if it were feeling some nameless grief similar to blind rage – and an anguish for which there was no cure in the whole world.

'Perhaps he's killed someone,' said Bernt. 'He's broken out of the byre and got loose again.'

'Let's go home. I don't want to stay here any longer.'

'You're a silly old woman and a cry-baby. If he comes here, I'll take my catapult and hit him on the forehead with a stone so he drops dead on the spot.'

'You'll miss. You didn't even hit that thrush in the rowan just now.'

'It flew away before I had time to take aim.'

I had seen the thrush quite calmly swinging on the branch while Bernt aimed and it didn't fly away until it was frightened by the stone whizzing by. But I didn't bother to argue with Bernt, because then he would perhaps be cross and hurt me.

'If he doesn't drop dead on the spot, then we'll climb up on that big rock over there. I'll help you.'

Bernt picked up a dead branch and waved it fiercely about.

The bellowing and roaring beyond the trees increased, crashing and echoing from all directions. You could hear individual human voices, terrified shrieks. Clearly a raging struggle was going on in the shelter of the shaggy trunks of the spruces. But suddenly the hideous noise was cut short and it was so quiet we could hear the light rustle of a bird's wing quite clearly as it swept by, then its sorrowful little call in the darkness of the foliage. For a moment we waited breathlessly for the noise to start again, but the silence persisted.

'I'm going home,' I said. 'My feet are cold.'

Bernt reluctantly put his catapult into his pocket and we set off homewards.

As we came out on to the road near home, some workmen's boys came rushing past, shouting loudly.

'Come on,' said Bernt, running in the direction of the byre. 'Something really has happened.'

I am used to adapting to Bernt's will, and I was also curious. I followed rather sluggishly, with a bored expression, so that Bernt should realize I found his eagerness silly and that I was really quite uninterested in the whole affair.

'Hurry!' he shouted, turning round. 'Why are you dawdling so?'

A tightly packed crowd was standing in a circle in front of the barn, just looking. Kuri Mari was there in her black silk hood and striped apron, and Riika the farm girl with her crooked peering face, Hämäläinen with his bowed back and rolling eyes, Uncle Georg with his moon-shiny beard, Uncle Heinz with his black eye-patch, the workers' children and many more. There was also an unfamiliar black horse there with a tangled unbrushed mane and forelock that fell right over its eyes, nosing at one of the roof supports. It was harnessed to a high four-wheeled wagon filled with all kinds of rags and bundles, bunches of straw sticking out between them.

A warm moist smell of blood struck us. In the middle of the circle two men in ragged white coats were busy doing something big and hideous. They were Harakka the slaughterer and his assistant.

They had hoisted Bull up on to a cross-beam. The flayed bluish-red body looked terrible. The legs had been amputated at the knee joints and the head had been cut off. At the ragged throat dangled blue-black threads of coagulated blood, still dripping. The ground underneath the hanging body was covered with blood, in some places shining bright red, in others glistening stickily and dark as tar. The assistant was doing his best to scatter something over the flayed hide. He folded it up like a rug with the pink damp side outwards and then flung it up on the wagon. The decapitated head was lying on a wooden crate, also flayed and scalped, so it was almost unrecognizable. Only the horns and eyes were real.

Then Harakka stepped up to the hanging body and thrust his knife right up to the handle into the navel. Then he slit open the belly with one long cut upwards and downwards. The entrails fell out like a huge multi-coloured bunch of fruit. Some of them looked like mother-of-pearl balloons, others like gigantic slugs or fungi, the colours shifting in dark red, brown and olive green. The skein of intestines was like a tangle of pale intertwined snakes held together by a thin lace-like veil, trembling and shaking as if alive. When the slaughterers leant over the pile and tried to get hold of it, the entrails slid out of their hands like fish.

Steam was rising faintly from the gutted body. Thin, scarcely visible veils of smoke hovered here and there like spiders' webs and dissolved as you watched them. Bull's spirit was parting from his body and floating upwards to gather and shape itself gradually up there in the clouds.

The Grown-ups were standing round talking in low voices to each other about something I couldn't grasp. Their faces were solemn and dignified as if they were at a funeral. Only the butchers remained untroubled, occasionally shouting something to each other in loud voices, laughing and swearing, as if they didn't care what it was they were doing. When one of the spectators got in their way, they angrily pushed him aside and went on without looking up from their work.

'Him's dead now,' said Kuri Mari. 'Poor Bull. But 'twas indeed quite a handful for two men.'

Uncle Georg was trying to explain something. He was sputtering and snorting, as if his mouth were full of bitten-off beard hairs he couldn't swallow. He was pointing here and there with his stick, but I couldn't understand what he was saying. He was obviously making these signs in order to put a seal once and for all on Bull's death and protect us from the forces still threatening us from the butchered body. Uncle Heinz was clutching his cloak round him, pulling in his chin and thrusting out his craw like a condor.

'Yes, him were old and nasty,' commented Hämäläinen, rolling his eyes. He took his pipe out of his mouth and spat out a stream of dark brown juice among the lumps of blood on the ground. 'At our age, a man can't do it no more, see!'

I went closer to the gutted corpse and looked inside. It was quite hollow and empty. You could have crept inside it and hidden as in a boat, only it was so horribly dark and slippery and the ribs could be clearly seen outlined on the inside of the walls. Something rather like a thick piece of hose hung from above.

Then the assistant started cutting up the stomachs. Bull had a number of stomachs and the man stuck holes in them with the knife as into giant blisters. But no young goats came out of them, or any gobbled-up children, only a greenish brown mess rather like the filling in a cushion. Meanwhile, Harakka cut loose the intestines, then wound them up in just the same way you wind up a hosepipe. Bull's intestines were terribly long and seemed to go on for ever. Suddenly they split – perhaps the knife slipped and cut a hole in them. A dark brown, almost black fluid welled out and formed little channels on the ground. However, Harakka didn't mind his hands getting soiled, but went on winding up the intestines and then throwing them behind him. It all looked so horrible that I couldn't bear to watch any more.

Bernt was standing in front of the crate where the head was enthroned, looking at it. I went over to him.

'Look, they've cut out his tongue,' he said. 'And the ears have been cut off too.'

It was weird standing so near that head. I had only to stretch out my hand to touch that golden ring still dangling from his muzzle. The head was much larger than I had imagined. I could easily have sat up between the horns as on a swing. The mouth was closed so that you couldn't see inside it, but the lips and corners were covered with blood-stained froth. Beside the head lay a pale oblong object that looked mostly like a peculiar sea creature. But then I saw that it really was Bull's tongue, covered with barbs and warts like a sea-urchin.

'Look at the way he's staring at us,' said Bernt. 'He can't talk, but he's thinking and can still see. Heads cut off like that can live a long time after they've been separated from the body.'

I shuddered. The glaring eyes in the skinless face, which was just one single open raw surface with arteries drawn in finely branched violet patterns, were truly horrible. I suddenly saw them slowly turning and fastening on me.

'He's looking at me,' I whispered to Bernt, retreating cautiously to one side. 'I don't want to stand where he can see me.'

'What are you afraid of? It's only a head. It can't do

anything to us when it has no body.'

'It might bite!' I said, moving even further away so that I was almost looking at it from the side. But however much I changed position, the eyes kept following me without the head changing position. Sometimes it could use only one eye, but it kept its eye on me the whole time. A great red tear glimmered in the corner and the deep blue iris was dark and moist. 'You see? He's crying,' I said.

'That must be because it hurts so much. You can be sure he's suffering dreadfully at the moment. Just imagine lying there like that with your head cut off, flayed and scalped, your tongue cut out and your ears cut off – watching your body being cut to pieces. Not being able to move and yet understanding exactly what's happening to you.'

I shuddered again. The punishment bestowed on Baal was certainly of the kind you simply daren't imagine yourself involved in. I saw his face twitching as he tried to twist it into crying, but wasn't able to. The bloody tears welled more and more from his eyes and made their way in little channels down the raw cheeks, drops falling from his nostrils and mouth and running down through the cracks in the crate. Underneath was a dark red sticky pool.

'How long until he dies?'

'He'll be barely conscious in an hour or two's time,' said Bernt. 'Heads of snakes and fish usually live longer. I know a boy who was bitten by a snake head two days after he had cut it off. He forgot to look out – but then he took an axe and chopped off the finger and lived.'

'What if it never dies?'

'You mean Bull's head? No, that'll be dead before nightfall. He can neither eat nor drink.'

I didn't understand, but I asked all the same. 'Do you think he's very hungry and thirsty now?'

'Can't you see it in him?'

'What do you think the worst thing is?'

'Thirst, of course. A burning thirst in his lips and throat. But it's impossible to quench it, because all the water would run out there at the back through the cut throat and he wouldn't be able to keep the tiniest gulp inside him.'

'But perhaps we should give him a little to eat and drink all the same?'

'You can try. But it's a waste of time.'

'I daren't. He'd just want to eat us up. He might bite my arm off if I went too close to his mouth.'

'He doesn't eat people. Wait, I'll give him a little hay.'

Bernt crept up to the cart and pulled a wisp of hay out of the nosebag. 'Here you are,' he said, holding it out so that it tickled Bull's muzzle.

Bull's eyes glimmered wildly and hungrily. He tried to open his mouth and part his lips, for a moment exposing his dirty yellow teeth. But he managed only to take a stalk or two into his mouth and they half stuck out between his lips. His eyes again took on that glassy expression you couldn't make out, and he went on staring intently at me.

'He can't chew any more,' said Bernt.

'Try poking it into his mouth. Take a stick. Here!'

Bernt took the stick out of my hand and tried to push the hay in. But the head refused to part its teeth. We had to take another stick to try to force open the jaws, but Bull stubbornly kept them tightly shut. Bernt managed only to poke the hay between the gum and lower lip, where it stopped like a plug of chewing tobacco.

'He doesn't know it's hay. He can't taste anything because his tongue's been cut out.'

'I think we must first give him something to drink. You said he was most plagued by thirst. Look how wildly he's staring at the water-bucket.'

That was when the horrible thing happened. As I put the bucket down and leant forward, I turned my back on the wooden crate and didn't notice I'd gone too close to the bull's head.

I suddenly felt it snapping at me and clamping a flap

of my jacket between its jaws just above the belt. I wanted to straighten up and run away, but I couldn't – I seemed to have grown into the wooden crate, and all the time I could feel the head pulling at my jacket so that my belt tightened at the waist and squeezed my chest. I began to scream.

Through my tears I could dimly see all the faces turning towards me and expressions of annoyance gradually changing to expressions of astonishment. The head pulled and pulled. Soon I wouldn't be able to hold out against it any longer.

Then I saw nothing but darkness. As if at a distance I heard my own screams, felt the crate tipping over me and something large, sticky and cold nosing at the back of my neck.

I don't know how I was set free. I suddenly found myself a long way from the crate, a lot of hands holding me and taking me away. I could walk again and nothing was pulling at my back.

'Be quiet!' shouted Uncle Georg, threatening me with his stick.

'It was only a nail in the crate. That's nothing to cry about,' said someone else.

I was so ashamed I daren't look anyone in the eye. When they let me go, I stood a long way away behind the others so that I could no longer see what was happening inside the circle. But not even then did I feel really safe. Supposing Bull's head were to rise up in the air and fly after me! No doubt it would be safest to get as far away as possible from that horrible place.

As I walked slowly up the slope to the stables on my way home, I could see the whole crowd collected round the remains of Bull. The head was still lying on the crate, its jaws open, trying to explain something. But Uncle Georg quietened it every time with a blow between the horns from his knobbly stick.

In the end, Herakka stepped up with his axe swinging in his hand, grabbed one of Bull's horns with the other hand and disappeared into the circle with the head.